Searching for Justice

by

Carolyn Rae

The New Horizons Series

Searching for Justice

Contact Information: info@thewildrosepress.com

Cover Art by *The Wild Rose Press, Inc.*

The Wild Rose Press, Inc.
PO Box 708
Adams Basin, NY 14410-0708
Visit us at www.thewildrosepress.com

Publishing History
First Edition, 2023
Trade Paperback ISBN 978-1-5092-4375-4
Digital ISBN 978-1-5092-4376-1

The New Horizons Series
Published in the United States of America

"I don't want to talk about legal stuff." Joe's face came closer. He kissed her. His lips were warm and sweet. Then he deepened the kiss. She responded, clutching his strong, firm shoulders. He pulled her closer, pressing his broad chest against her breasts, making her heart beat faster.

When they finally broke apart to breathe, he smiled. "You taste even better than I imagined."

And then his lips, those fascinating lips, met hers again, softly at first. When she leaned into his kiss, he squeezed her shoulders and increased the pressure on her mouth.

This time she didn't hesitate, but threw her arms around his neck and kissed him with all the feeling she'd been trying to push down. Closing her eyes, she reveled in sharing the kiss. His tongue slid between her lips and roved over the inside of her mouth, daring her to join. And she did, enjoying every swipe and push.

He gazed into her eyes. His smile pulled at her. Still holding her hand, he caressed her shoulder. "I know I invited you for a drink, but I want to tell you. I'm very attracted to you, and I'd like to take this further tonight. I hope you feel the same way."

Wow. He must be picking up vibes from her. She picked up his cup and took a sip. "Let's forget about work tonight, but tomorrow, it's back to being opposing counsel."

"I'm okay with that," he said.

Entranced, she waited, her pulse thrumming.

Other Wild Rose Press Titles by Carolyn Rae

Searching for Love: The New Horizon Series, Book 1

Tossed aside in favor of her sister, a determined Valerie Trumbull reluctantly teams up with her ex-fiance's brother, Matt Larson, to hunt her missing sister south of the Texas border. Valerie expects him to be a jerk like his brother, but Matt compliments her and says he finds her sexy. When she awakes on a narrow cot in their Mexican prison cell, she is warmed by his arms around her.

Attorney Matt Larson is attracted to Valerie, but she argues constantly with him about his plans to find her sister. Valerie also disappears, and he sets everything aside to find her. Then she's delivered, half alive, to his office in a wooden shipping crate, and he realizes how much she means to him. Can they manage to compromise while searching for her sister?

Dedication

This book is dedicated to my husband, Jack, who encourages me.

Acknowledgments

My critique partners, Pepper, Jessa, Sabine, Sue, and Shanna, and the members of DFW Writer's Workshop, who have read and listened to my chapters and made suggestions for improvement.

Chapter One

Expecting a contentious deposition this sunny September morning, Joe Morales stepped from his Lexus and walked toward the red, brick building in Dallas's West End.

Footsteps sounded behind him. He turned. His opponent for district representative was close behind, his eyes drilling into Joe's.

"Hey, Morales, I'm Cash Carter—"

"I know who you are." Carter's grinning face was all over billboards and TV ads for the election to replace a dead representative for the Texas House. With his expensive haircut and charm, Carter was going all out to win. "I don't have time to talk to you now."

His opponent's outrageous TV ads annoyed the hell out of Joe. He gritted his teeth. It was frustrating to keep denying the false allegations. How could Carter afford all those ads?

After moving from San Antonio to help his mother with his ill father, Joe had discovered the district's Hispanic and African American residents needed someone to champion their causes in the legislature and the city.

Dallas developers wanted to raze older apartment buildings and small houses to build expensive homes and apartments the current residents couldn't afford. As a kid in San Antonio, he'd lived through that before his family got displaced and moved to Dallas when he was in high school. He'd talked to the Dallas zoning commission about that happening here.

Carter stepped closer. "We could set up a public debate."

That was a good chance to win over voters. "Sure, have your campaign manager call mine to set it up. We can discuss the issues people are interested in."

"The main issue is your running for office. As an attorney only a few years out of law school, your lack of experience stands out like drops of water drooling down the side of a glass."

Joe blinked. Man, the guy had nerve. "I'm a legitimate candidate with over five thousand signatures, and I paid the filing fee."

"You've got little legislative experience. You've only lived in Dallas a bit longer than the required year." Carter pointed his thumb at his own chest. "Now, as a candidate for the more popular party, I have an excellent chance of winning. Your running against me is an embarrassment. You're going to lose, so why don't you withdraw now?"

Joe laughed. "Not a chance. Bet you're worried you'll lose."

"I suggest you withdraw…or…things could get ugly." His opponent's voice was disturbingly quiet, but Joe heard every word.

Scowling, he straightened his shoulders and stuck his chin out. "Let the voters decide. I don't have time to argue now." Turning, he strode to the building's rear entrance without looking back. He walked inside, letting the door clang shut behind him.

Ugly? He grimaced. What would Carter resort to

next? Joe checked his watch. He needed to review his notes before Richard Black's deposition. The builder hadn't done anything to cause a homeowner's yard to develop a sinkhole.

Walking across the granite floor, he passed a tasteful arrangement of gladioli and mums on the counter and waved to the clerk behind it. The smell of coffee wafted from the little cafe down the hall, reminding him he hadn't had any this morning.

After a quick trip to get a cup, he inhaled the bracing aroma of the steaming brew and headed to his office. A few sips of coffee helped as he opened the door to his office suite and walked across the brown-carpeted reception area he shared with his fellow attorney, Matt Larson.

Anne, their young, brunette legal assistant, sitting at her cherrywood desk, smiled, then resumed typing on her keyboard.

Matt, Joe's dark-haired partner, stepped out of his office and leaned against the paneled wall. "Something on your mind?"

Did his aggravation show? Joe nodded. "Cash Carter is damaging my campaign."

Matt opened his office door wide. "Come on in."

After closing the door behind him, Joe leaned against it. He grumbled about his recent conversation with his opponent.

Matt sat behind his paper-strewn desk and listened. He fingered his well-trimmed beard. "The guy sounds threatening. You might want to consider a bodyguard. Cash Carter may deny any connection to his Uncle Frank Carter's organization in San Antonio, but I'm sure he's tied up with him."

"Carter wouldn't dare attack me before the election."

"I wouldn't be too sure," Matt said. "Remember, Frank hired the hoodlums who kidnapped my wife and delivered her in a box to your office while she was in San Antonio seeking her sister."

"Sorry you two had to go through with that." Joe checked his watch. "I need to get ready for my deposition. Want to join me for lunch at Bobby Joe's Barbecue afterward?"

"Sounds good," Matt said.

Joe walked into the conference room and studied his notes. A large window flanked the conference table. Hearing a noise outside, he turned.

A tremendous crash startled him. Something hard smashed against his face. Whatever it was landed with a clump on the table. The pain was almost unbearable but soon subsided into a throbbing ache. Plopping into the nearest chair, he rested his head in his hands.

"What was that?" Anne stood in the doorway, her hand on her chest. "Sounded like a window breaking." She stepped inside. "Oh, my gosh."

The window had a large jagged hole. Large and small pieces of glass littered the polished oak floor. A brick on the edge of the table had shoved a pile of papers into disarray. Joe looked out, scanning the area. No one was visible near the building.

Beside him, their legal assistant stared at the brick. "Oh, my. What if someone had been sitting there? I'll call maintenance to clean it up."

"Damn," Joe said. "I was standing there, and I got hit."

She looked at him. "Oh, you're hurt. You need to

see a doctor."

"Right now, I want you to please call security and the police."

She returned to her desk, sounding anxious as she made the calls.

He rubbed his temple and leaned over to read the note taped to the brick. Big, black letters said "WITHDRAW FROM THE RACE." Bitter bile churned in his stomach. He clenched one hand into a fist and then relaxed it. Blood smeared his fingers, giving off a coppery smell. He wouldn't back out of the election. However, he would postpone the deposition and let the police handle this.

Matt stood at the doorway. Joe waved his hand over the table. "Don't touch anything. There might be fingerprints." Holding his hand against his temple, he headed back to his office.

A few minutes later, Bob Adams, the building security representative, walked into their office suite. After Joe explained what had happened, Bob said, "I'll check outside to see if anyone's hanging around the building." He left.

Ten minutes later, a police officer arrived. Joe's head really hurt, but he led the officer to the conference room, introduced everyone, and explained what happened. "My opponent for state representative could be behind it. I don't have any proof, but I wouldn't put it past him."

The officer slipped the note into an evidence bag. "I doubt we'll get fingerprints from the brick." He put that into another bag, then walked over to the window. "I'll look outside for footprints, but I doubt I'll find anything on the pavement. I'll also check with your building security officer for any video from the surveillance system and let you know. It's probably a long shot though."

As the officer left, Matt fingered his bearded chin. "Maybe we need to start recording the incoming calls."

"Good idea," Joe said. "Anne, can you call someone to set up our phones for that?"

Anne nodded. "I'll check on that right away."

Joe headed to the bathroom to wash the cut on his forehead.

****

Earlier that morning, Kayla Walker scanned the long list of interrogatory questions from Attorneys Larson and Morales, then turned to the tall, slender paralegal she shared with the lawyer in the adjoining office. "Beth, can you get to work on answers to these questions this morning?"

"Sorry, but I have to prepare a divorce decree for Laura next door. That will take all morning, and I need to prepare a list of questions for the deposition she's having this afternoon. I should be able to get to the work you need later this afternoon."

"I understand. Please bring me a draft when you've finished." After checking her e-mail, Kayla found a request to turn in the number of billable hours she'd worked and a note saying she needed to increase the amount next week. As the newest attorney in the firm, she wondered if that meant she had to keep billable hours high to keep her job.

Frowning, Kayla drafted a letter in another case and sent it to the printer in the workroom. Since Beth was busy, Kayla walked down there. Tapping her feet, she smoothed back her brown hair, waiting while the printer spewed out a lengthy print job for another attorney. Finally, her letter was ready, and she left it on Beth's desk to address an envelope.

Kayla gritted her teeth. She'd thought she was lucky to land this job at a medium-sized firm. Working for a firm with politics, favoritism, sharing a legal assistant with another attorney, and the constant pressure to rack up billing hours hadn't been as fulfilling as she'd expected, but she was confident she was well prepared for the deposition later this morning.

She didn't enjoy defending tax cheats against the IRS. How did seven years of effort in school and her passion for justice turn into defending loopholes for people determined to pay for mansions and limousines but avoid taxes to keep the roads maintained?

Maybe she'd check with an employment agency during her lunch hour, but now she needed to head out for her eleven o'clock deposition to question the developer her client was suing.

If only the conference room here was available, she'd have the deposition here, but the other, more-prominent attorneys had already scheduled the room for all the times Joe Morales was available. And as new kid on the block, she had little clout.

She'd get to the deposition early and scope out her opposing attorney. She wanted to win this, her first big case, for her client, a former neighbor who'd asked her to take his case. His new house was in danger of falling into a sinkhole developing in his backyard. A squirrel darted in front of her car, and Kayla slammed on her brakes to avoid hitting it.

A few minutes later, she drove into the parking lot for the red, brick building where the deposition would be held. Parking her three-year-old Toyota Camry next to a black Lexus, she wished she could afford one like it. Between her condo's fifteen-year mortgage with high monthly payments and her student loans, her bank account stayed low, but she'd save interest in the long run.

After getting out of her car, she straightened her navy suit jacket and brushed her skirt. Holding her head high, she walked into the building, her heels tapping on the pink-and-gray granite floor. She found the suite with "Larson and Morales" on the door and stepped inside. Her heels sank into a caramel carpet as faint clicking noises sounded from the brunette legal assistant's keyboard. Brown leather chairs sat below a pretty landscape painting.

She envied these attorneys in their small firm. Sure would be nice to work in a situation like theirs. But that wouldn't happen until she'd won sufficient cases to attract enough clients to break even.

Down a hallway, a police officer in a black uniform stood talking to two men, Larson and Morales, she assumed. Had they been burglarized? Or perhaps they had contacted a policeman for information about a criminal case.

One attorney turned to face her. Wow. With dark, wavy hair, he was the best-looking man she'd seen in a long time. His dark-brown suit fit well and complimented his tan skin. For several seconds, he focused his brown eyes on her. He seemed interested, and that ignited an answering spark within her. A quick glance assured her he wore no wedding ring.

She'd been too busy to socialize much, but here was a guy she'd like to get to know better. There was a fifty-

fifty chance he was the attorney she'd be arguing against. With her luck, he'd be the one.

He must be dependable to make it as an attorney. His air of confidence showed he kept control of things. It remained to be seen whether he expected people to follow his orders without question and hand over everything he asked for.

Kayla stood there. She'd wait until they finished with the police to introduce herself. She looked forward to the deposition. Her client needed justice, and she'd wring enough answers from the builder to make a good case.

The sharp-looking attorney faced the officer and pointed to the conference room. "Cash Carter, my opponent for state legislature, spoke to me earlier this morning. He said if I didn't withdraw, things might get ugly." The officer wrote on a notepad.

The attractive attorney then walked over to her. "I'm Joe Morales." His face lit up with a friendly, welcoming smile. "Please excuse me for making you wait, but we've been busy with another matter. May I help you?" His voice was deep and rich.

He must think she was a prospective client. Too bad she'd be arguing against him in court. "I'm Attorney Kayla Walker. I'm here for the deposition."

He held out his hand. His grip was warm and firm, and he smiled as he shook her hand. "Nice to meet you, Kayla. I'm sorry, but we'll have to postpone it."

"Why? It's almost time for it to start. My client and the court reporter should be here any minute."

"It's too bad you drove all the way here for nothing. I know your time is valuable." He turned to their legal assistant. "Anne, didn't you call the opposing attorney?"

She nodded. "I tried to call but was unable to reach her."

He stuck his hand in his pocket, jingling keys or coins. "I'm sorry you weren't notified about the change in plans. I received a threat this morning, and someone threw something through our conference room window. It may be connected to my running for office—"

"I see," Kayla said. "That sounds serious."

A man wearing a uniform with "Building Security" embroidered on the pocket walked into the reception area. "I checked but saw no one outside the back of the building. Whoever it was is long gone."

The officer faced the security guard. "Do you have surveillance cameras focused outside the building?"

The guard nodded. "I checked. All that camera caught was a brief shot of an arm throwing something. Could have been a man or a woman."

The policeman turned toward Joe. "We'll check the fingerprints on the note against AFIS. I'll let you know if we find a match." He strode out.

Kayla raised her eyebrows. Politics could be dirty business. Why wasn't the cop taking this more seriously? Even though Joe Morales was her opponent in court, she didn't want anything bad to happen to him.

Joe walked back to the legal assistant's desk. "Anne, please call Richard Black and the court reporter. Advise them not to come because the deposition will be rescheduled."

As Anne picked up the phone, Kayla hurried over to her desk. "No. Wait." She faced Joe Morales. Time to fight for her client's rights. "You shouldn't postpone the deposition for a little thing like a hole in the window. Our clients and the court reporter will be arriving any minute."

Joe Morales shook his head. "I'm not subjecting those people to sitting in a vandalized conference room."

"But my client's house is sinking. He may lose everything. He needs to be paid enough money to get his house shored up or moved to another lot. Time is of the essence."

Anne looked at Joe questioningly.

"Hold off for a minute," Joe said. He faced Kayla, his lips clamped together. "That wasn't just a rock someone threw. It was a brick, a large one with a nasty threatening note. I was hoping we could settle the case this morning without going to court, but your demand for half a million dollars is ridiculous."

Kayla stepped closer. "My client is in danger of losing his new house and everything in it. He has a right to be compensated. We need to settle this case quickly so he can afford to fix his property before his house and all his possessions are destroyed."

Joe shook his head. "None of the houses in his development have had any problems. Sinkholes happen all over Texas. Richard Black is not responsible for a natural anomaly."

"He should have done core samples on each lot. I intend to ask him about that."

"I'm sure he did, but I'm not holding a deposition today. It could take several days to replace the window, and my schedule is full."

Kayla's chin jutted out. "You shouldn't let a little thing like a broken window keep you from doing your job."

Joe's eyebrows angled close together. "It's not my responsibility to hold a deposition you asked for at your convenience."

"My convenience?" She glared at him. "I agreed to present my client on the date your legal assistant specified, even though I wanted it sooner. His home's dangerously close to collapsing. He'll pay to get it fixed, but he needs to be reimbursed."

Joe rubbed at his temple. A streak of blood showed up from under a dangling lock of hair hanging over a flesh-colored bandage.

"Oh, my goodness. You're bleeding. You need medical attention. Okay, let's have the deposition one evening later this week."

Joe swiped at his forehead. The blood on his fingers seemed to surprise him. "I'll take care of this in a moment, but let me ask you something. Do you want to pay extra for a court reporter to work at night, that is, if you can even get one to work evenings?"

"Never mind that. I'll take care of getting a court reporter."

"The earliest I can manage is Friday at eight."

Kayla frowned. That would make for a long night. She'd push for earlier. "What if I have another engagement Friday?" Of course, she didn't. She'd been too busy working to socialize much, but Joe Morales didn't need to know that.

"Take it or leave it," he said.

Kayla frowned. "Wait a minute. Can't we start earlier, say, about six o'clock?"

"I'll agree to six thirty, but that's as early as I can manage. Anne, call Richard Black to see if he'll be available. Then call building management and get them to fix the window."

"I already did that, sir," Anne said.

Kayla walked out. That attorney with a movie-star face and million-dollar smile could be so annoying. She clenched the fingers of one hand into a fist, then called her client and told him not to come. Joe Morales had gotten the best of her this time, but she was ready to unload all her research on sinkholes on him. She'd question the developer about taking core samples from her client's property before building there.

Chapter Two

Back in her office, Kayla straightened papers on her wide, walnut desk, venting some of the energy she felt toward Joe Morales. Her office might not be spacious, but she loved the wide window with a view of the park across the street, particularly when she was stressed.

Since it was almost twelve, she looked forward to lunch in the park. She could spend her lunch hour away from the office phone, with only the warbling of birds and rustling of squirrels. She directed Beth, her legal assistant, to print out the temporary orders prepared earlier to show her divorce client at one o'clock.

A few minutes later, Beth brought her the day's mail. "A gentleman is waiting to see you in the reception office. He acts like he thinks he's rich and important. He wanted to follow me, but I insisted he had to wait until you agreed to see him."

"I'm glad you did. I can't have men bursting in on me without notice." Surely, Joe Morales wouldn't come here, but her heart skipped a beat. "What's his name?"

"Clay. He said he was an old boyfriend, and you'd be glad to see him, but I wasn't sure, so I made him wait."

Kayla groaned. "I broke up with him months ago." Thinking their relationship was exclusive, she hadn't realized he was a player. She'd felt hurt, but after the breakup, she realized she was better off without him telling her how to dress and suggesting she see a hairstylist he knew.

It was bad enough her mother did that too. Back when she lived at home, her sister, Denice, spent a lot of time rolling her hair on sponge curlers. However, by the time Kayla had finished her homework, she was too tired to curl her hair. In the mornings, she barely had time to coax a comb through it. Now, busy all day with clients, Kayla still wore a simple hairstyle so she could get ready faster in the mornings.

Kayla wished she had parents who showed her love and appreciation, instead of fawning over her sister. She'd often heard Mom giving her sister tips to attract a boy she was interested in. Her mother complained because Kayla didn't wear the latest styles like her sister, but Kayla wore suits to look professional.

Mom was always harping on her to meet some nice guy and get married. Well, Kayla had her own plans for her life. She wanted to get some important cases, make a name for herself, and get promoted.

Why on earth did Clay want to see her now?

"Let him wait while I look over the mail."

Clay burst into her office, his massive frame enveloped in an expensive-looking silk suit. "What do you mean, let me wait? Why keep me waiting while you take care of mail? You can do that later."

Beth stood there, her mouth open. "I did ask him to wait."

"I'm sure you did, but I'll handle him." She faced him. "Clay, you can't just barge in and interrupt me. If you have something to say, tell me and then leave."

Clay touched his artfully moussed hair. "I have a new look. How do you like it?"

"I think I prefer the clean-cut hairdo you had as a college football player."

"Well, I'm moving up in the world. I'm running for state legislature as Cash Carter. I'll win for sure because I'll impress people with my honesty and forthrightness."

Remembering he'd boasted about cheating on a few college exams, Kayla almost choked on that.

He continued. "I'm sorry about what I said when we broke up, but I need a classy lady at my side. I want to hang out with you now. And as a bonus, you can be my attorney if I need one. What do you say?"

"It's not going to happen, Clay, or should I call you Cash, since that's your political name. I've moved on and have a good job." She picked up her pile of mail. "I need to deal with this now." She concentrated on showing him a determined face, but he remained standing there. "Have a nice day." She opened the first letter, hoping he'd leave.

He stepped back. "You've changed. You're more determined. Guess that comes from being a lawyer and arguing in court."

"Look, Clay, I'm busy. Beth, my assistant, will show you out." As she opened the second letter, he finally turned and walked toward the outer office door Beth was holding open.

Clay scowled. "You'll regret turning down the opportunity to be with me. I know plenty of influential people who might offer you a better position."

She did want to work for a different firm, but not with his help. "Bye, Clay."

She glared at him, waiting for him to leave.

"I'll see you around." Finally, he walked out, his footsteps sounding a little louder than usual. He slammed the door of the outer office as if to say she hadn't seen the last of him yet.

"Man," Beth said, "I bet you're relieved to see him go."

Kayla nodded. "If he comes again, tell him I'm with a client."

Beth smiled. "Got it."

When Beth brought in the divorce temporary orders, Kayla checked them over. Good. Everything was spelled out as it should be in readiness for the hearing. After Beth left to go work for Laura, Kayla barely had time to eat her sandwich and enjoy a Coke.

At one, Kayla met with her client Rose Witherspoon. "Your name is so similar to the movie star's."

Rose laughed, her light tone contrasting with her distraught expression. "When my husband introduces me to a new friend, the man usually asks if I'm related and could I introduce him to Reese Witherspoon."

"What do you say?"

"I tell them the only thing we have in common is being female and having the same last name."

Kayla held out the documents her assistant had prepared. "These are the proposed temporary orders I'm presenting to your husband's attorney. Look them over and tell me if you want anything added."

Rose examined the documents, brushed tears from her cheeks, and helped herself to a tissue from a box on Kayla's desk. "My husband agreed to let me stay in the house until the divorce, but I need a job. Half of our assets and child support won't be enough to pay expenses for my daughter and myself for very long."

Kayla studied Rose. It must be awful to be cast aside

with a daughter to take care of. "Do you have any college or experience in the workforce?"

"I have a few college credits in English literature, but I'm not trained for much of anything." She wiped her eyes. "Now I'm sorry I didn't get a job doing something before I had my daughter, but Larry wanted to have children right away. He wanted a son, but he hasn't paid much attention to Sally."

Rose deserved to be free of such a man. Kayla vowed to get the best settlement she could for her. "While you'll still own half of the house and one of your two cars, half the bank account won't last long. Since you don't have any experience, in addition to child support, we can ask for funds for you to train for some profession."

"In college, I'd thought about changing my major and becoming a nurse, but Larry wanted to get married right away, so I quit." She wiped her eyes again. "Now, I wish I hadn't."

Her client must have really loved Larry to do that. Kayla couldn't understand how love could make one give up a goal. And as exciting as Joe Morales seemed, she would never allow him or a boyfriend or a husband to talk her into that. It was too late to advise Rose on that, but Kayla wanted to help her now. "Nurses are in demand in this area. At Texas Women's University, you can become a registered nurse and graduate with a degree."

Rose looked up expectantly. "That sounds good. Where can I find out about that?"

Kayla checked Google for TWU, wrote their number down, and handed her a slip of paper. "Call this number for information."

"Thank you. I feel better about the future now. I'll call as soon as I get home."

"I'll include a provision for the necessary funds in your divorce decree. Prepare an estimate of all the college expenses you'll have. Then I can support your request for money when I speak with your husband's attorney."

"I will." Rose stood and actually smiled.

Kayla handed Rose a card. "Here's the business card from an attorney down the hall, who might need a receptionist. Maybe she'll consider you for the position."

Rose beamed. "Thank you so much." She smoothed her blonde hair. As she walked out, her steps seemed lighter than when she'd come in.

Kayla called her attorney friend, Laura. "I just sent one of my clients to you to talk about working for you. I'm handling her divorce, and her soon-to-be ex has agreed to pay her child support, but nothing more. She hasn't much experience—"

"Then why are you sending her to me?"

"The legal assistant we share can't keep up with all the work you give her."

"You can't expect her to get it out faster. She has to keep up with all the work for both of us."

"You kept her all this morning on your client's divorce decree, so I had to wait to get my documents printed. Maybe you could use a receptionist to do some of your typing. You handle more divorce cases than I do."

"I'm not sure I need a typist full-time."

"But couldn't you use someone part-time?"

"I don't know. I'll have to think about it."

"My client's soon-to-be ex said she would keep the

house, but she wants to go to college in Denton. She needs money for that."

"Okay," Laura said. "I'll talk to her, but I'm making no promises. What are you doing Friday night? We could go someplace for dinner."

"Sorry, but I've got a deposition scheduled for then. How about Thursday night?"

"Sure, but what jerk of an attorney schedules depositions on a Friday night?"

Kayla explained the situation.

"So, is he young, single, and good-looking?"

Kayla laughed. "You're always trying to fix me up. Yes, Joe Morales is actually all three." But she'd seen other tall, dark, and handsome men who didn't attract her like he did. He was charming and friendly, but she needed to keep him at arm's length. She had to make good as an attorney. She didn't have time for romance.

"Where shall we meet Thursday night, say, about six thirty?" Laura asked.

"How about Outback? I love their coconut shrimp."

"That's good. And you can tell me more about Joe Morales."

Kayla laughed. "He's very argumentative." She swallowed. "I hope I can get enough evidence to beat him in court. I'll see you tomorrow."

****

Thursday evening, Kayla and Laura sat in a booth beneath a picture of a huge sandstone mountain and ordered coconut shrimp. Under the picture, a caption said, "Formerly known as Ayer's Rock, now named Uluru." Curious, Kayla Googled it and read from her phone, "What you see covers an area of 3.3 square kilometers and rises 345 meters above the plains. It's the surface expression of a much larger volume of rock, laid down in an inland sea during the Cambrian Period about 500 million years ago, but it got tilted up."

Laura stared at the picture. "That's impressive, but tell me about Joe Morales. What's he like?"

Kayla drew in a deep breath, leaned forward, and lowered her voice. She didn't want the couple with two teenage kids passing by to hear. "His smile is enough to light me up inside. I find him very attractive—not smart since he's the opposing counsel on one of my cases, an important one against a developer we're suing for a sinkhole on my former neighbor's new house. If Joe Morales and I seem too friendly, that could cause us both problems."

Laura grinned. "You're right about that, but tell me more. What's he look like?"

"He has brown, wavy hair I'd like to get my hands into. He didn't seem that tall until he stood close to me, and I had to look up to meet his brown eyes. He seemed friendly and nice, until I insisted on having the deposition this week. However, he is a smooth dresser and seems like a confident attorney."

Their food arrived, and Kayla picked up a coconut-encrusted shrimp. She savored the buttery shrimp and the sweet taste of the pineapple dip that came with it.

Laura leaned forward. "So maybe after the case you share is over, you might ask Joe if he'd like to meet for lunch—no, that's too obvious. Tell him you have two tickets for a play or a baseball game, if he likes those."

"I'll have to figure out if he's interested before I do that. I'm not going out on a limb and risking embarrassment." Her heart fluttered at the possibility he might be as attracted as she was. Wouldn't that be something?

"I guess you'll have to wait and see."

Joe seemed appealing. He certainly was loyal to his client. She'd like to get to know him better—away from court and legal wrangling—but that wasn't likely now. Besides, he probably had a girlfriend.

She and Laura shared a piece of Outback's delicious carrot cake. Kayla hoped tonight's dinner wouldn't add any pounds. Maybe Joe probably preferred dainty and fragile-looking women rather than outspoken professional women. After saying good night to Laura, Kayla decided Joe would probably use charm and expect a woman to follow his suggestions.

Friday morning, Beth walked into her office with a huge vase of pink and white roses. "Someone must like you a lot."

"Set it on my desk," Kayla said. She sniffed the flowers, her favorite kind. She fingered a white rose petal. It was so soft. As much as Joe had seemed interested in her, would he send her flowers? They barely knew each other. Besides, they were on opposite sides. Sending her flowers wouldn't look good if anyone at his firm found out.

But it would be a nice gesture. Kayla smiled. As the paralegal returned to her desk in another room, Kayla pulled out the card. It said, "For the sweetest and smartest woman I know, love, Clay."

She groaned.

She'd dated him during the summer for three months before her friend Cathy told her he was dating three other women on the nights he'd said he had to work late. Kayla had been a fool. Mad at him for treating her this way, she'd told him she didn't want to see him anymore. Of course, he'd asked why. Gritting her teeth, she related what Cathy said.

"That's not true for two of those women. I only took Lucy out to lunch because she worked for a business I wanted to cultivate as a client." All the time he told her that, he was fiddling with his phone and not looking her in the eye, like she didn't even matter to him.

She didn't give him time to persuade her. She'd stood up straighter. "I don't believe a word you said. Leave, and don't call me again."

Now the man himself walked in. Oh, no. She wanted to tell him to go jump in Lake Ray Hubbard or better yet a manhole. Clay could be charming at times, but he was also determined to get his way. Now promoting himself as Cash Carter, his tactics even included threatening Joe Morales. No way would she get back with that loser.

"Thank you for the flowers. They're lovely, but I already told you I don't want to see you. Don't come here again, and don't give me flowers."

"I knew you'd like them. I thought you could enjoy them after I take you out to lunch at Ruth Chris Steak House. I know you love their food. They have their eleven-ounce, filet mignon on the lunch menu."

"You don't give up. You sound like their best PR person, but I have a client coming at one, and I brought my lunch today."

He reached over to take her hand. "Can't you call your client and reschedule for one thirty?"

She pulled her hand away, but he continued, "That would give me plenty of time to feed and entertain you."

"No. I'm not going anywhere with you. And I won't change my client's appointment time."

"But, sweetheart, I so want to enjoy your company

again. After all, didn't you say we could part as friends?"

Kayla didn't remember anything of the sort, but Clay kept talking. "And what's wrong with friends having lunch together and catching up on old times?"

Kayla stood. "I have work to do. Goodbye, Clay."

He paused at the doorway. "When you eat your lunch, I'm sure you'll regret turning down a steak."

"Beth, will you please see Mr. Carter out so he won't get lost. Have a nice day."

"I don't need a damn assistant to show me out."

She sat and bent to study a paper, watching over the top of it to be sure he left.

He frowned, turned his back, and walked out.

She sighed. *How can I be so strong in court but not send this jerk packing right away?* Now, Joe Morales would have taken her at her word and left. He appeared forceful and confident, traits she admired. His smile had warmed her immediately, and the way he looked at her had set her heart beating faster. Too bad they shouldn't socialize while on opposing sides of a case.

Kayla opened the first letter in her pile of mail. It had the return address of Larson and Morales. They'd better not postpone the deposition again. She pulled out the document.

Larson and Morales were now representing Rose Witherspoon's husband, making it two cases she and Joe Morales had in common. Kayla sighed, and her stomach churned. She didn't need any more stress today.

Chapter Three

Kayla checked her watch. It was eleven thirty now. Might as well take an early lunch hour. After grabbing her lunch bag from the refrigerator in the break room, she headed for the park.

The sweet gum trees sported yellow, orange, and red leaves, adding color to the darker, green leaves of trees not ready to change color. The metal bench she usually sat on seemed cold. Trying to ignore the hard metal seat, she scanned the Internet and found a job listing agency for legal work. Her sandwich seemed dry and tasteless. She made a list of three midsize firms that seemed attractive. Luckily, Dallas had many law firms to choose from that paid well.

Friday evening, Kayla dressed for the deposition in her gray pinstripe suit with a tailored white blouse. She'd like to have Joe see her in a pretty dress, but she needed to look professional. After checking her briefcase one last time, she made sure her list of questions to ask Richard Black was there. Her folder had printed information about sinkholes and the likelihood of them appearing in certain areas of Texas.

It was still warm as Kayla walked confidently toward the red, brick building. If Richard Black hadn't obtained core samples for the property, she'd nail him with failure to properly survey the land before building and win compensation for her client.

Fifteen minutes later, she sat at Lawson and Morales's walnut conference table beside the new plate glass window. Bright fluorescent light illuminated an impressive array of materials at the head of the table. Joe Morales's legal assistant brought in another stack of papers and straightened everything into neat stacks.

This was going to be an uphill fight. Girding for battle, Kayla set down her thick file folder and laid out her sheet of questions. Joe Morales walked in, looking handsome in a charcoal-gray suit and white shirt that emphasized his nice tan. He made the introductions in his mellow, deep voice, then stated the date and listed those present. The court reporter's fingers flew over the keys.

Joe Morales nodded at Kayla. "The floor is yours, Counselor Walker."

She stood and glanced at Joe Morales's winning smile. She would not dwell on how attractive he looked. She would concentrate on what to say next.

After taking a deep breath, she stared at her opponent's client. Contractor Richard Black looked uncomfortable in his smooth-fitting suit. He'd probably prefer wearing jeans and a knit shirt. "Mr. Black, did you take core samples from the property where you built Thad Thayer's house?"

"I believe so. I took core samples everywhere to see what type of soil was there."

"Can you state unequivocally that you took a core sample from his property?"

"I'm sure I must have."

"Then I expect you to produce a report of the core sample from that property."

"I'll check."

"Are your houses built on soil made up of clay, sand, and limestone rocks? That's where most sinkholes occur."

"Much of Texas has that type of soil. It's expansive soil which swells when it absorbs moisture."

"But does your development have the type of soil I mentioned?"

"I'm sure some of it does."

Kayla sat and made notes. "Does your development have problems with the sewers and drains?"

"Some, but I have workmen fixing that."

After she asked Richard Black a few more questions, Joe Morales broke in, his voice sounding smooth and persuasive. "If your client would agree to a reasonable settlement amount, we could avoid going to court."

Kayla spoke up. "My client won't be satisfied with less than half a million dollars."

"That's ridiculous," Joe said. "My client says the house isn't worth more than $350,000."

"But he's had it decorated and painted just the way he likes it. The furnishings may not fit as well in another house. And all the anxiety he's suffered, wondering if part of his house is going to sink in the night while he's sleeping, is worth at least another $150,000, which adds up to half a million."

"There's no way we'll agree to that."

"Then we'll see you in court," Kayla said. She picked up her materials and stood.

"Can you wait a few minutes?" Joe Morales asked. "I'd like to talk with you after the court reporter leaves," Joe said as the woman packed up her equipment.

"It's late. Surely we can talk about it over the phone

on Monday."

"You don't need to stay very long, but I always like to know a little bit about my opponent's lawyer before meeting him or her in court." He smiled.

Kayla studied his determined chin with an interesting cleft. However, his brown eyes now looked more interested than argumentative.

After everyone else but his legal assistant had left, Joe said, "How about some coffee? I can have Anne make us some."

What was he up to? Was he going to try to talk her down about the amount of the settlement? She wasn't going to be persuaded to change her mind, but if she got to know how he thought, she might be able to negotiate better with him later. "That would be nice, but I don't want to argue about the settlement amount tonight."

He ran his fingers through his wavy brown hair. "Fine. We can talk about other things. I'll see if there's any coffee in the break room." He left the room but returned a few minutes later with two steaming mugs.

He settled in a chair at the head of the table. "Would you like some pie with the coffee? I can have some delivered from the building's coffee shop, which also opens to the street. They have apple, lemon, and chocolate with a meringue topping."

"I'd like chocolate."

He punched a number on his phone and ordered chocolate and apple pie to be delivered.

"So, how long have you lived in Dallas?" she asked.

"I moved to the city a little over a year ago, long enough to run for the Texas legislature."

"I see. Won't that cut into your ability to take care of your clients?"

He shook his head. "The Texas legislature is only in session during the spring of even-numbered years, but I can still be available to my constituents at my office in Dallas during the rest of the time."

"Why do you want to run for office?"

"Hispanics in my area need a representative who pays attention to their interests. They want more state money for schools and more free parks." He leaned forward, obviously interested in his potential constituents' welfare. "Their concerns need to be addressed."

His legal assistant brought in two pieces of pie on paper plates.

"Thank you, Anne. You needn't stay any longer. I'll lock up."

She walked out the door, and soon, Kayla was savoring the rich chocolatey pie.

Joe's eyes twinkled. He smiled, making her feel like she was sitting outside in the sunshine. She caught herself watching his lips as he bit into a forkful of pie.

What would he be like on a date? What on earth was she thinking? He was her opponent in two cases. Thank goodness he couldn't read her mind.

He met her gaze. "Wait a minute. Your last name is Walker. Are you related to David Walker? As a professor at SMU, he's been a mentor to me since before he became Speaker of the Texas House."

"He's my father. Strange he never spoke of you."

Joe clapped his hand on his forehead. "I should have realized that before now. David's a lawyer, and you are too. I'm surprised he hasn't mentioned you were. So where did you go to college?"

"I did my undergraduate work at University of

North Texas, but I went to UT for law school."

"Like you, I went to UT—for my undergraduate degree. My parents paid for that and for my first year at SMU law school, but I had to get a job to pay for the rest when my younger siblings started college. Is this your first job right out of law school?"

She nodded. "At the time I felt I was lucky to get hired by a medium-sized law firm, but as a new hire, I have to share a paralegal with another attorney."

"How many lawyers are at your firm?" Joe asked.

"Twelve."

"My partner, Matt, left the large firm he worked for and went out on his own. I'm glad he took me in as a partner. Last year, I let him work out of my office in San Antonio for a murder case he had there, so he was happy to offer me a place here. Luckily, his client was finally acquitted."

"That was generous of you. Do you still have an office there?"

He laughed. "I couldn't keep up with another office five hours away."

"What brought you to Dallas?"

He explained about his ill father, then asked, "Have you always lived in Dallas?"

"I grew up here."

"My family moved here from San Antonio when I was in high school, but I set up my law practice in San Antonio. It's a shame we never met before. So, what's there to do for fun around here now?"

"The clubs in Deep Ellum have some good music. And I like dancing and playing pool."

"Maybe I could challenge you to a game of eight ball." He grinned. "Bet I could beat you."

She leaned forward. "No way. I'd love to challenge you to a game at a bar, but that's not a good idea. Our clients may doubt our loyalty."

Joe was interesting to talk with. It would be nice to spend another hour doing just that, but it had been a long day. She stifled a yawn.

"Sorry, I'm keeping you up. Let's call it a night," he said. "I'll walk you to your car."

He scanned the parking lot. "You can't be too careful at night in Dallas."

Once she was behind the wheel, she let the window down.

He patted her arm, sending a delicious tingle all the way up. "Good night, I'll see you in court when the case comes up."

He smiled. "Drive carefully now. By the way, I'd like to have your private number also. If you hand me your phone, I'll put in mine."

She liked the way he cared for her safety. He was so handsome, and his voice continued to charm her. Besides, he was interested in having her cell phone number. She pulled her phone from her purse. As his fingers closed over hers, imparting a spark, she squeezed his hand, then pulled away. She didn't need to be attracted to him, but she wouldn't let that stop her fighting to get justice for her client.

About to hand the phone to him, she remembered she had client numbers on it. She pulled the phone back. "I'll just give you my card. It has my cell phone number in case my clients need to talk to me after business hours." She took the phone back, careful not to touch his fingers, and fished in her purse for a card and held it out. He took it, his fingers touching hers, zinging her with another spark.

After she rolled the window up and started the engine, he walked to his car with a smooth, easy stride. At least he didn't have pressure from the head attorney to turn in enough billing hours to prove his worth. Time for her to get busy hunting for another job.

Later that evening, as she was updating her resume, she received a text.

—*Did you get home okay?*—

She replied back.

—*Yes.*—

That was thoughtful of him. She had enjoyed talking with him over pie. And when he smiled at her, she'd felt warm all over. Too bad they were on opposing sides. He probably could date any woman he wanted. She, however, had better concentrate on her career.

Saturday morning, she typed up three letters asking for appointments. Two she sent by e-mail as requested, the other she sent by regular mail.

****

Saturday morning, Joe was seated at his cherrywood desk, sorting piles of paper and trying to prioritize tasks. He gazed out his window at the nearby golf course. It would be nice to take a walk with Kayla, holding her hand on a similar green lawn in a park. Thinking of Kayla's curves, he figured she'd feel nice to hold, too.

Even her scent was enticing. He admired how passionate she was about getting justice for her clients. She seemed dedicated to doing her best for them. She'd be loyal to her friends, too. He didn't know why his thoughts were rambling in her direction. Too bad she was forbidden territory. Otherwise, he could really go for her.

He tapped his fingers on his desk. He had to keep

remembering she was his opponent and nothing more. He needed to concentrate on winning the case against her client.

Outside, a bunch of robins gathered on the nearest green, pecking for food. He wished he could be out there instead of facing the pile of files on his desk. He was tired of handling so many criminal cases. Many of his clients showed up dressed sloppily and didn't smell good. He often had to lend clients one of his ties and put an arm around their shoulders in court to make them look relatable. Thieves and burglars usually didn't pay very well, either.

The phone rang. His mother was on the line. Moving here to help his mom with his ailing father had its advantages. Something interesting was always going on in Dallas. He was glad the energy-sapping summer heat didn't last as long here as it did in San Antonio. He'd had to struggle to purchase his home, although it was older and needed fixing up when he bought it. Since then, he'd kept it in good repair.

"Hello, dear. Your father took the car, and I don't know where he is. He's been gone for two hours. I'm sure he's gotten lost."

"Mother, I'm so sorry you have to deal with that." Joe hated that his dad, whom he'd looked up to for so many years, was losing his memory and making his mother worry. "You need to hide the keys. He shouldn't be driving."

"I know. He can't remember what day it is half the time, but he always seems to remember I keep the keys in my purse. I was washing my hair in the shower when he walked out the door. It wasn't until I dried off and dressed that I realized he'd taken the car. I don't want to put him in a memory care place, but I can't seem to control him, especially when I leave the house for my bridge group or my charity meeting."

Joe sighed. "Does he have his phone with him?"

"I called several times, but he isn't answering."

Joe rubbed the back of his neck. "Do you want to have the police issue a senior alert?"

"He'd be so upset if the police stopped him. He gets confused sometimes. I'm not sure he'd understand why they were stopping him."

Frustrated, Joe glanced at his desk, covered with papers and folders. He needed to get that done, but his father came first. He hoped his dad hadn't had an accident. "Do you want me to drive around Coppell to see if I can find him?"

"Oh, would you? I'd feel so much better if you were looking for him."

Joe sighed. "I'll see what I can do. Talk to you later, Mom."

Twenty minutes later, pushing down the tightness in his stomach, Joe drove along Bethel School Road near his folks' home. Maybe his father had gone to Duck Pond Park. After pulling into the park, Joe saw his parents' pale-blue Chevrolet. It sat alone and empty. Joe stopped his car beside his father's and got out. A metal bench sat nearby, but his father was nowhere in sight.

Joe wandered between oak and beech trees, calling, "Dad, where are you?" All he heard were chirping birds. A redheaded woodpecker with black-and-white-speckled feathers flew to a tree and poked his beak into the bark, probably looking for bugs. A slight breeze ruffled Joe's shirtsleeves as he walked along a leaf-strewn path near a wide, rippling creek. Still no sign of his father.

At one place where stones made a path across the wide creek, Joe glanced along the rocks to the other side. Joe's father sat on a large rock. With graying hair and several days worth of scruff on his face, he'd rolled up his pants, but they looked damp. His shoes lay beside him.

He threw pieces of bread toward the ducks puttering nearby, but most of the bread landed in the creek. Little mottled fish with gaping mouths clustered, fought for the morsels, and roiled the water into cloudy ripples. The loaf of bread his father held was almost full. It looked freshly opened.

"Hi, Dad. What are you doing over there?"

"Can't you see? I'm feeding the ducks."

"Did you tell Mom where you were going?"

"I think I did, but I can't remember for sure."

"Dad, you need to tell her when you go someplace. Sometimes you get lost, and she needs to know where to look for you."

His father brushed back his gray hair and frowned. "Don't talk to me like I'm a child."

"Dad, you know how Mom is. You were gone so long she got worried."

"Worried? What for?" his father demanded.

"With the three of us gone, y'all are empty nesters now. She doesn't have anyone but you to fuss over now." Joe grinned and shrugged. "Maybe she worries some younger woman might latch onto you and run off with you."

His father chuckled. "Really. At my age, that's not likely." He twisted the end of the bread bag. "What do you want now?"

"Come on back across the creek, get in your car, and follow me to your house. On the way, let's stop and get some chocolate milkshakes."

"I'm enjoying just sitting here. We can do that some other day. The sun feels good on my bare feet."

"Tell you what," Joe said. "Why don't I come over there and steady you so you won't fall off the stones on the way to the bank?"

His father glanced around and then back at Joe. "Okay."

After crossing the creek, Joe picked up his father's shoes, stuffed with his socks. Joe took his dad's arm and pulled him up. "Let's go home now."

Luckily, the stones in the brook were close enough for Joe to stand behind his father and steady him as they walked to the other side.

After opening the driver's door of his dad's Chevrolet, Joe gestured for him to get in. Once his dad was seated behind the wheel, Joe said, "Now follow me. I'm driving to the nearest McDonald's to get us some chocolate milkshakes."

As Joe pulled into the McDonald's, he wondered if Kayla loved milkshakes too. Then he looked up and saw his dad had kept on going. Joe backed out and followed his father. When he got to the street for his parents' house, Joe clicked on his turn signal, but his father's car kept moving slowly down the street.

Joe pulled up behind his dad and honked several times. Finally, his father stopped. Joe drove alongside, lowered his window, and pointed back the way they'd come. His dad looked confused, so Joe got out and motioned for him to roll the window down. "Look, Dad, you passed the house. I thought you were going to follow me, but I turned into McDonald's, and you just kept on going."

"Guess I had my mind on something else, son."

"Be sure to follow me now." Joe trudged back to his car. His dad, who'd taught him to fish and handle a gun, was really in bad shape. Joe needed to have a long discussion with Mom. As he pulled into his parents' driveway, his father's car kept going, then stopped. Finally, he backed up and pulled his car into the driveway beside Joe's. As they walked into the house, his dad said, "Sorry, I didn't recognize the house at first."

His mom, her graying hair in a neat ponytail, faced her husband, her hands on her hips. "Howard, we've lived here twelve years. How could you forget where we live? I was really worried about you."

"I'm tired," he said. "Think I'll go to bed."

Joe handed his father his shoes and socks. Without another word, his father took them and left the living room.

Joe collapsed on the couch. His stomach felt unsettled as he dreaded the conversation he needed to have. "Mom, I need to talk to you about Dad. He didn't remember how to get back to the house. He agreed to follow me, but he's showing signs of dementia. You need to take him to the doctor."

His mother shook her head. "He's just tired. That's what made him forgetful, I'm sure."

"No, Mother. It's more than that. I suggested getting milkshakes—you know how he loves chocolate milkshakes. I told him to follow me. When I got to McDonald's, he kept right on driving. And then he didn't recognize your house and kept on going down the street. You need to keep the car keys away from him."

His mother shook her head. "But he loves driving that car. He'd feel like I was treating him like a child."

"Do you want his car to be listed on roadway signs as a Silver Alert for people to call the police if they see his car?"

She sighed. "Surely, it hasn't come to that."

"I'm afraid so. Give me one set of keys, and keep the other somewhere he won't find them."

She left the room and returned with some keys. "He's taking a nap. I had to fish in his pants pocket to find them."

"If you lose your keys, you can always call me."

She hugged him. "Thanks for finding him."

"Mom, you probably ought to get a part-time health professional to help."

"I don't need anybody like that. Besides, it would cost a lot. And I'm not going to put him in some nursing home. I married him for better or worse, and I'm taking care of him."

"Then, you need someone to keep an eye on Dad so you can get out once in a while. If you need money, I can help out."

"He'll be okay here by himself if I take the car. Besides, I don't need to be going out a lot."

"Yes, you do. Going places with your friends will keep you active. And promise me you'll take Dad to a doctor sooner rather than later?"

"What will I tell your father? I'll have to tell him something."

"Just tell him it's time for his annual checkup."

"But he just had one two months ago."

"I doubt he'll remember. Just make the appointment and take him there. Be sure to tell the doctor ahead of time what to look for."

His mother sighed. "Okay. I'll do it."

"I've got to go now, but consider getting some help. I'll talk to you later." Walking out to his car, Joe hoped he'd gotten her to think about the future. He didn't want her wearing herself out taking care of his father. After laying the groundwork, maybe next time, he could get her to see how much better it would be to have help.

****

All that week and the next, Kayla waited for replies from law firms with positions open. Two sent letters saying they were not interested. That hurt. She thought she'd looked good as a candidate, but obviously those firms found someone they liked better. Maybe she'd hear from the other soon.

By Friday morning of the following week, tired of waiting and wondering, she picked up her copy of the letter she sent the third firm she'd applied to, shut the door to her office, and called them. They transferred her to the human resources department. A woman answered and asked her to wait a moment.

Put on hold, she listened to loud music, alternated by comments about how hiring that firm could solve her problems, and drummed her fingers on her desk for six minutes. Finally, a Miss Bowen answered and asked what she wanted.

"This is Attorney Kayla Walker. I sent in a letter saying I was interested in the position your firm has open. May I schedule an interview?"

Shuffling sounds of rustling papers came over the phone. "I cannot find your letter."

"I'll send another. Whom should I address it to?"

"Put it to the attention of Ms. Carla Bowen. Oh, wait

a minute. Here it is. Sorry, I spilled coffee on it and can hardly read it. When did you send this?"

"You should have received it on Monday of last week."

"Mr. Bowen already interviewed six applicants and doesn't want to see any more. I believe he has two women he is considering. Besides, he only answers letters from very experienced attorneys. I have lots of work today, so if you don't have any more questions, it's time to say goodbye." *Click.* The woman disconnected.

Damn. Kayla crumpled her copy of the letter and tossed it against the wall. That's all she needed to make her day disheartening. Her shoulders slumped. Now she'd have to start all over again. She felt empty inside. Didn't anyone want to hire an attorney who'd graduated cum laude? Was she stuck at this firm?

She wasn't going to give up. She checked the Internet for more positions and wrote down the information.

After a long afternoon catching up on work, she ate a late supper and watched TV. That evening, she typed up two more letters and sent them off by e-mail. Hopefully, someone would see them first thing Monday morning.

She took a shower, wrapped a towel around herself, and walked into the bedroom. As she closed the blinds, she caught sight of a shadow near a tree. Was someone out there? She grabbed a robe. After putting it on, she lifted one slat and peeked.

The shadow was still there. It sent shivers down her spine. She picked up her phone, pushed Dial, then looked again. The shadow was gone. Should she call 911 now? Better check again. She flicked on her security light. The whole area was bathed in light, and no one was visible. She checked the locks on the front and back doors and set the alarm. If someone broke a window, the alarm would ring.

She got ready for bed and slid beneath the sheets but couldn't get comfortable. It took a long time to fall asleep.

The next morning, Kayla stepped outside and looked for footprints but found none. Feeling unsettled, she headed for her office.

Chapter Four

On Monday at work, she tried not to think about the letters she'd sent. Instead, she tried to do as good a job as she could on the tasks at hand. She gave Beth a list of items to prepare for her next court hearing. Kayla wanted every document and fact at her fingertips while she was in court.

****

Standing on the podium in the large room he'd rented for his town hall meeting, Joe glanced at the foam poster board with his picture and his slogan, "Morales Will Work for You in the Legislature."

After gathering his notes, he rubbed the back of his neck. His campaign manager had suggested he give a brief biography about himself. He hated talking about himself. He wanted to talk more about the things he hoped to accomplish in the legislature.

He gripped the sides of the wooden podium and looked over the crowd. One gray-haired lady seemed to be paying attention, but a middle-aged man with tan-colored skin in the second row was checking his phone. An unsettled feeling filled his gut. Would the people believe him or think he wasn't experienced enough to be in the legislature? Then it dawned on him. He wasn't here to talk about himself. He should ask them about their concerns. And let them ask questions.

"What causes do you want me to bring up in the

legislature to help our community?"

A short, stocky man rose from his seat and asked, "What can you do about the developers who want to raze our houses and build apartments and shopping malls?"

"The only developer I represent builds houses on vacant land, but I can understand your concerns. If a developer requests a zoning change, he or she must notify all who live within two hundred feet. But if you rent, only the landlord will get a notice. You can check with your neighbors to see if a change has been requested. As citizens, you can attend the hearing and protest to the Dallas City Council and the Dallas Zoning Board of Adjustment."

While he was speaking, Kayla slid into a seat in the back row. His heart beat faster. He was glad she'd come, even though she didn't live in his district and didn't seem interested in politics.

A woman with glasses and dark, wavy hair raised her hand. Joe motioned for her to speak.

"I'm Maria Hernandez, and I live near the park at Joe Pool Lake, but it's always so crowded I can hardly spread a blanket for a picnic with my family."

"There's a large area of undeveloped land that could be added to the park," Joe said. "I'm a good friend of the speaker, and I believe he'll support me if I push for a bill proposing that to be read, discussed, and voted upon."

Several men sitting on folding chairs made comments or asked questions. Luckily, those were easy to answer. They seemed enthusiastic and kept him busy answering questions.

"Does anyone else wish to speak?" Joe asked.

No one raised a hand. "Well, then, that's all for tonight. I hope you'll vote for me." Everyone clapped.

People rose and pushed chairs back. The sounds of shoes sliding across the wooden floor accompanied their filing out.

Two men and a woman walked up to speak to him. One man asked about highway repairs. "The farm-to-market road I travel to work has lots of cracks and potholes."

Joe said, "Think I've traveled that road a time or two. I can talk to whoever is in charge of state highways if you folks send me to Austin."

One man nodded. "Hope you make it." The three turned and headed for the door.

Kayla stood at the open door, waiting to speak to him.

Stepping out from the podium, Joe smiled and waved at the last attendee to leave. His campaign chairman gathered up flyers, the easel, and the foam poster board with his picture and his slogan and walked out to the parking lot.

Joe picked up his notes and walked toward her. "I'm surprised to see you here. I'm glad you came." A cool breeze chilled his ears as they walked outside.

"I'm not really into politics, but I wanted to hear what you stand for. I was impressed with the way you connected with the people. I think you showed you were really interested in their concerns."

He couldn't help smiling. "Thanks. I appreciate that. It's nice to know you are interested in me and my views."

"A good citizen should know about the issues before voting, and they seemed to want to discuss them."

When they walked outside, he caught a breath of her perfume, smelling of gardenias. Only two cars sat in the parking lot, his Lexus and Kayla's red Camry. "Hey, would you like to go somewhere for coffee?" he asked.

She smiled. "I'd like that. Where shall we meet?"

Joe headed for the driver's side of his car. "Why don't you suggest a place?"

She walked over and stood between the cars, silhouetted against the dark sky with the moon and only a few stars showing. His car leaned to the right. That was strange.

Kayla stared at his wheels on the right side. "Why would someone do that?"

He hurried around his car and stood beside her. Both tires were slashed and flat. "Damn it all." He gripped his hands into fists.

Kayla bent to study one tire. "This is awful. I didn't see anyone hanging around your car when I walked in."

Joe rubbed the back of his neck. "Must have happened while I was talking." He scowled. "I'm sure Cash Carter's behind it. He wants to upset me so I'll do poorly in the TV debate tomorrow."

"If it is Cash, he's playing dirty politics, but you need to work even harder on preparation. Think of all the accusations he might make, and have a good comeback ready."

He pulled out his phone, took pictures, and groaned. "I only have one spare." He called his insurance company and arranged for a tow.

"I'll be glad to wait with you for the tow truck and drive you home."

He smiled at her. "You don't need to. The tow truck driver can take me home."

"But you'd have to wait until he unhooks your car and puts it in the garage. You must be exhausted after answering all those questions."

"Thanks. I'd appreciate it. And I'll enjoy your company while I wait."

"I'm glad it isn't cold. I remember the time I had to wait for a tow. It was cold and seemed like he'd never come. I must have waited half an hour in the cold."

"That must have been awful. Wish I was there to keep you warm—but I didn't know you then." His intent brown eyes met her gaze, and his comment warmed her heart. "I hope riding in the tow truck warmed you up."

She nodded. "It felt good to thaw out." She glanced back at the meeting room. "Those people seemed interested in asking questions and talking to you. I hope that means they'll all vote for you." She pointed down the street. "I think that's the tow truck coming."

After the tow truck hoisted his car up, he told the driver where to take it and climbed in her car. As he leaned closer to direct her to his house, he caught another whiff of her perfume. She smelled of gardenias.

As she parked in front of his house, he said, "Thanks for bringing me home. The least I can do is offer you coffee or something stronger. Would you like to come in?" He gazed at her, hoping she'd say yes. He wished she'd want to stay, but she hardly knew him or how much he wanted to hold her.

****

Kayla glanced at him. He'd made her really feel welcome at his town hall meeting. He'd be a good legislator, and might be a strong manager in his office and at court. But he seemed to be enough of a gentleman to take no for an answer to anything more. She relaxed. "Coffee sounds wonderful."

He unlocked the door of his one-story house and stood aside. "Ladies first."

She stepped into a polished oak entryway and looked around. On the right, gold pillows decorated his brown leather couch. Several magazines lay strewn on the coffee table. He loosened his tie, draped his jacket over the easy chair, and dropped his tie on top. After laying her wrap beside his, she walked toward the couch with small piles of printed pages lying haphazardly on the couch. Should she move them so she could sit down?

"Please don't touch those. I have them exactly how I want them. I have a few investments I keep track of, and I'm looking to invest in other stocks." He picked up one stack and set it on the coffee table. "Have a seat." He gestured to the couch.

He walked toward the doorway of a small kitchen. "Do you want coffee, tea, hot chocolate, or something stronger?"

"Hot chocolate would be nice."

"Your wish is my command." He smiled, bowed, and turned toward the kitchen area.

He wasn't so amenable in legal matters, but he was being the perfect host. She liked the way he strode confidently into the small kitchen. A family picture sat on the bookcase, showing him with a younger brother and a sister. Joe was definitely the most handsome young man she'd met in a long time.

A few minutes later, he set a mug of hot chocolate and a paper napkin on the coffee table, next to the stack of magazines, and placed his mug of hot chocolate on top of the stack. Then he moved another stack of papers to the far end of the couch and sat beside her, even though an easy chair sat next to the couch. He faced her and grinned. "You're nice to be with when we aren't arguing a case."

"Thanks," she said. His gaze met hers, his interest making her pulse speed up. She liked sitting this close instead of facing him across a table. She set down her mug. "This is good."

He took hold of her hand, causing it to tingle. "Thanks. Actually, I make my own mix with dark chocolate cocoa and coffee cream. I fell in love with hot chocolate in Spain and wanted something similar. I didn't like anything that was in the stores. Did you know the Olmecs used fermented cacao for rituals and medicine, but the Mayans, who came after them, mixed the paste with water, cornmeal, and chilis, seasoned it with flowers or vanilla pods, and then drank it hot. Later, Aztecs in Mexico drank it cold."

"I don't think I'd like it that way."

"Well, when Cortes left Mexico, he took cacao beans with a mortar and pestle and returned to Spain. Europeans tried adding things like cinnamon, sugar, and milk to the drink."

"I like it better sweet, and yours is especially good."

"Thanks." As he sipped his hot chocolate, he kept looking at her over the top of his cup. The light in his brown eyes called to her. Some crazy whim made her want to ruffle the waves in his carefully combed dark hair. She caught herself leaning toward him again and tried not to succumb to the sizzle sensitizing her body.

She rose and walked over to a bookcase. She pointed to a family picture set on the top. "Tell me about your siblings. How old are they?"

"Diego is seventeen, and Angelina is twenty-two. She just graduated, enjoys being single, and is looking for her first job."

"So, I guess growing up, your family spoke

Spanish?"

He shook his head. "Many people in San Antonio speak Spanish, but my parents wanted me to speak English well, so they insisted we speak it at home. However, when we went to our grandparents' house— they lived a couple blocks away—they only spoke Spanish, so we did too. *Abuela* let me help her make cookies and some typical Mexican dishes."

"My grandmother," Kayla said, "was an excellent cook, but my mother had to take cooking lessons after she got married. One day, I asked Nana—that's what we called her—to show me how to make something. She took the bowl, poured in a handful of flour, and stirred it. She did things so fast, I couldn't learn anything from her. That's why I agreed to take Family and Consumer Science in school after my father suggested it."

He stood and stepped close to her. "I bet you're an excellent cook now."

"I hope so."

He set his cup down on the top of the bookcase and took hold of her hand. Conscious of the way he was smoothing the back of her hand, she felt the pull of his sensuous smile. His face with those interesting lips moved closer. What would it be like to taste them? She wanted to move closer, put her hands on his shoulders, and kiss him, yes, kiss those forbidden lips that kept calling to her.

This was all wrong. She couldn't give in to her attraction to him. "Let me know if you need any more proof of my client's damages."

"I don't want to talk about legal stuff." His face came closer. He kissed her. His lips were warm and sweet. Then he deepened the kiss. She responded, clutching his strong, firm shoulders. He pulled her closer, pressing his broad chest against her breasts, making her heart beat faster.

When they finally broke apart to breathe, he smiled. "You taste even better than I imagined."

And then his lips, those fascinating lips, met hers again, softly at first. When she leaned into his kiss, he squeezed her shoulders and increased the pressure on her mouth.

This time she didn't hesitate, but threw her arms around his neck and kissed him with all the feeling she'd been trying to push down. Closing her eyes, she reveled in sharing the kiss. His tongue slid between her lips and roved over the inside of her mouth, daring her to join him. And she did, enjoying every swipe and push.

He gazed into her eyes. His smile pulled at her. Still holding her hand, he caressed her shoulder. "I know I invited you for a drink, but I want to tell you. I'm very attracted to you, and I'd like to take this further tonight. I hope you feel the same way."

Wow. He must be picking up vibes from her. She picked up his cup and took a sip. "Let's forget about work tonight, but tomorrow, it's back to being opposing counsel."

"I'm okay with that," he said.

Entranced, she waited, her pulse thrumming.

He pulled back to look at her and grinned. His fingers dipped beneath the neckline of her blouse and smoothed the top of her breast. He gazed at her intently, as if waiting to see if she welcomed that. It felt so exciting, she just smiled and leaned closer.

He undid several buttons, then lifted her breasts and kissed the tips of both, right through her lace bra. They swelled and tingled.

He caressed both breasts as if they were precious and smiled. "You don't know how long I've wanted to touch you like this. I only hope…"

She couldn't help grinning. "I love it."

He unsnapped her bra and pushed her blouse open all the way and gazed at her. "Your breasts are beautiful." He kissed each one, then began to suck one, making it swell and sending a spark to her core. He suckled her other breast, sending a wave of excitement through her.

Seeing the delight in his eyes, she arched her back, pushing her breast into his eager mouth. She'd never been with a man who made her feel so excited, so wonderful, and so wanting more. Her whole body felt electrified. He took hold of her hand. "Stay with me tonight." His face seemed filled with longing to be close to her. He kept hold of her hands and waited. "Please."

She didn't want to stop now, not before she'd experienced more of his touch and all he was offering. She smiled. "Yes." She sounded breathless, but she didn't care. She walked with him to his bedroom.

Rust draperies hung at the window. He tossed a tan bedspread to the foot of the bed. He put his arms around her, kissed her again, and grinned. "I have you just where I want you, I hope that's where you want to be?"

She kissed him back. "More than anything." She kicked off her shoes. The soft rug caressed her feet.

He pulled her zipper down and shoved her skirt to the floor. After sliding her blouse and bra off, he kissed her breasts again. "I can't wait to rest my head on your lovely, soft breasts."

She smiled. "And you can as soon as we get rid of

these clothes." She unbuttoned his shirt and slid it off, then worked on his belt. Soon his pants slid down his slim hips to the rug, and he kicked off his shoes. His erection tented his boxers. She could hardly wait to feel it firm against her belly and then slide into her.

He peeled off his socks and took hold of her lace panties. "Pretty, but they need to go."

"So do these." She grinned and grasped the waistband of his boxers. Together, they removed the last bits of clothing and lay on the bed.

His firm chest pressed against her breasts, but he propped himself on his elbows to keep his full weight off her. He kissed her mouth, then laid a trail of kisses down her body to her navel. She moved his hand between her legs. "I don't want to wait seconds more for you to tease your way up my thigh."

He went straight to her core, touching her, setting her afire.

His fingers worked magic with her pussy. Soon the pressure built, and her tissues tingled. She squirmed in delight and grinned up at him. Oh, what he could do to her.

After opening a drawer of the bedside table, he pulled out two foil-wrapped packets. He took one condom and slid it on his enormous erection in a second. Her heart beat faster as she anticipated more to come. She felt his tip nudging her. Then he entered slowly, stretching her more and more.

He began a rhythm, which she enthusiastically joined. He pushed and she pushed. He gazed, and she met his look. He grinned, and she smiled. Exhilarated and on top of the world, she wanted this to last as long as possible. The pressure built again. And the tingling.

He gave a powerful thrust and took her up to a mountaintop, then zoomed over the edge for an exhilarating ride.

She felt him climax too and hugged him. He kissed her heartily. "You're more wonderful than I imagined you'd be." He laid his head on her breasts. "Mm, you feel so soft and warm. Please stay all night with me."

She cradled his head against her breasts. "Wish I could. I know this is a big city, not a small town, but someone might see my car parked here all night. We're on opposing sides in two cases. This was a mistake." She smiled at him. "A lovely one. Except, we can't do this again."

"Damn. You're right. We have to act professional until we're no longer on opposing sides."

She rolled off the bed and began dressing. He just lay there. "I like to watch, but I'd rather see you take your clothes off than put them on." He grinned.

When she finished, he slid into a robe and walked her to the door. He took her hand and squeezed it. There was that zing again. She shouldn't have let herself get attracted to him, but his smile kept pulling at her.

She couldn't resist giving him one last kiss before he opened the door. She put her arms around his neck. His mouth met hers in a long kiss, satisfying while it lasted, but leaving her hungry for more. Reluctantly, she pulled away. "Take care."

"Good night. Please text me to let me know you got home safely. And drive carefully so I don't have to deal with another lawyer from your firm." He laughed.

He was off-limits. But he looked like he wanted to pull her close again.

"I need to get home. Good night." She pulled her

keys from her purse and hurried out the door.

All the way home, she remembered how wonderful it felt lying in his arms and how she wished they could do it again soon, but they shouldn't. Not while they had opposing cases.

Now, if only he wouldn't flirt with her, she'd be able to act professionally when they were together.

After texting him, she lay in bed thinking of the exquisite pleasure she'd had. Was he thinking about her now? Maybe he didn't do long-term relationships. Was this merely a pleasurable one-night stand for him?

Chapter Five

A few days later, Kayla sat on a bench outside the Dallas courtroom, facing Rose Witherspoon. "I'm sorry. I tried, but I haven't been able to persuade the opposing attorney to convince your husband to grant you enough to finance four years at Texas Women's University. I forwarded the judge a decree granting expenses for all four years, but I don't know if he'll approve it. I've seen the order your husband's attorney has sent to the judge. On that one, your husband agrees to pay for two years of your expenses, but I'm hoping the judge grants one or both of the other two years' expenses." She'd hoped after he considered that Rose needed to be able to support herself, Joe might talk to his client about her client's need to get a nursing degree.

While sitting in the courtroom waiting for the hearing, Kayla heard Joe slip and call the judge by his first name. Immediately, he added, "I mean, Your Honor." Were they friends?

An hour later, after the judge ruled at the hearing for temporary orders, using more of Joe's provisions in the judgment than those Kayla had presented, she clamped her jaws together. Stunned, she gathered up her notes, feeling empty and defeated. Couldn't the judge see how unfair Joe Morales's proposed settlement rulings were to her client?

Following her tear-streaked client from the

courtroom, Kayla didn't feel much better, but she had to keep up an expectant face for the disappointed woman. "Rose, why don't you register for that nursing course? Maybe you can get a scholarship for the other two years."

Rose brushed at her cheeks. "After promising to love and cherish, I never thought it would come to this. He makes a good salary. It's not as if he can't afford it."

Kayla rested her chin in her hand. "They figure child support on the father's ability to pay. I'll check to be sure he'll pay the full percentage of his income as mandated. That should help with daycare expense."

As they waited for the elevator, Rose said, "Thank you for all you've done. I know you tried your best to get the full four years."

"You're welcome," Kayla said. "I wish we'd gotten a better outcome." She had tried her darnedest, but the judge had ruled mostly in Joe's client's favor. That settlement was so unfair. She gripped her briefcase so hard her knuckles whitened.

Joe and Rose's soon-to-be ex-husband walked toward the elevator. Rose looked away, but Kayla faced Joe. "Your client is shirking his duty to support Rose and Sally while she finishes four years of college."

Joe's eyebrows furrowed. "The judge has decided. If you don't like it, go ahead and appeal his ruling."

Kayla pointed a finger at Joe's chest. "Your client owes it to her to help her get a degree so she can provide for herself and their daughter."

Rose's husband glared at Kayla. "Don't talk about me as if I'm not here. My lawyer does what I tell him to do."

Kayla's chin jutted out. "Only paying for two years

of college is just wrong. Counselor Morales, you should be ashamed of yourself for letting your client avoid paying."

Frowning, Joe held up a finger. "My client has been more than generous by letting her stay in the house and agreeing to pay expenses for two years without even knowing how much they will cost. I'm looking out for his best interests. That's my job."

The elevator door opened, and Joe and his client stepped inside.

Kayla snapped her mouth shut. No one said anything. She touched Rose's arm. "We'll wait for the next one."

After they stepped inside the next elevator, the hot stuffy air seemed to press in on her. She couldn't wait until they could step out on the ground floor.

Okay, so sometimes life wasn't fair. This time Rose was getting a terrible deal.

As she and Rose walked toward the courthouse door, Kayla tried to swallow the knot in her throat. She'd tried but hadn't gotten what her client needed. "Would you like to stop somewhere for a cup of coffee?" Maybe that would reduce some of the sting from the judge's ruling.

Rose shook her head. "I have to pick up my daughter from daycare." She hurried to the door and walked away.

As Kayla climbed into her car, her phone rang. It was Joe. She didn't want to talk to him, but said hello anyway.

"You may not want to hear from me right now, but let's agree to disagree on today's case for now. After what we shared the other night, I hate to be at odds with you. I thought we could discuss the sinkhole case over a drink at a bar in Deep Ellum later tonight. There's a group playing there you might like to hear."

At any other time with any other man, that would sound interesting, but there was no way she would go out with him. Especially not since he'd trounced her in court. "Not only are you the opposing attorney for two cases of mine, but I can't believe you have the nerve to suggest that after encouraging the judge to approve such an unfair decree for my client."

"So that's a no?"

"That's correct. I don't want to meet you at a bar, tonight or any night. If there's anything we need to discuss concerning the sinkhole case, you can call me at my office later in the week. Goodbye."

****

Back in his office, Joe scowled. The heat in her voice had washed over him. If she'd stood near him, he'd have been singed. Damn it all, he still wanted to go out with her. He wanted to taste those luscious lips again, but she was having none of it. Why did she attract him so?

Okay, she was right. They shouldn't date until the cases they had in common were over. But after that he wanted to see her again. Wanted to hold her in his arms and kiss her. Wanted her in his bed. Wanted her to feel as strongly about him as he did about her.

Wondering how she really felt unsettled him. Was she merely mad about his client's refusal to pay for four years of college, or did she hate Joe because of that?

Should he have suggested his client agree to pay more? No, his duty was to get the best deal for Witherspoon. He'd fought for that, and the judge had signed the temporary orders in his client's favor. Why didn't he feel the usual exultation for winning out?

He and Kayla did have business to talk about, but he shouldn't have asked her out like it was a date. That was unprofessional. She might think he would talk her into reducing her client's claim for money to fix his property. Her heart was in the right place. She fought fiercely for her clients. That made her an excellent lawyer, one he admired. But she was a damn sexy one. He could hardly wait until they weren't on opposite sides. But would she still be antagonistic to him then?

She was definitely a strong woman. Before asking another woman for a date, Joe probably should consider the kind of woman he might want to associate with for longer than a few dates. It would be nice to have a woman who supported him and was congenial.

However, arguing with Kayla was strangely challenging. And when she wasn't arguing, she was interesting to talk to. Except the sinkhole case was coming up soon, and they'd be arguing in court again. Luckily, it would be after election night. He and his campaign helpers would spend the next two weeks knocking on doors, and he would focus on winning the election. He felt more comfortable meeting people one-on-one than speaking to large groups. He was always afraid he'd say something stupid.

Anne interrupted his thoughts. "Mr. Black is here to speak with you."

After his legal assistant ushered his client into Joe's office, Richard Black slid into a chair opposite Joe's desk. "So how are my chances of winning the case against me?"

"I can't promise anything, but I can make an excellent case for that sinkhole being an unpredictable force of nature."

"I hope that sinkhole is an isolated incident. I want to build a lot more houses in that area. Unless, of course, the legislature passes that bill to extend the area of Cedar Hill State Park. That will eliminate some choice available land for enlarging my subdivision. I'll vote for you in the upcoming election, but I hope that bill won't pass."

"Thanks for your support, but I won't decide until I know more about the issue and hear the arguments for and against."

Richard laughed. "You sound like a real politician, sitting on the fence until you see which way the wind blows."

"I'll vote for whatever appears reasonable and will benefit my constituents."

"I like that approach, but I hope you'll vote against that bill."

A week later, on a whim, Joe called Kayla and invited her to his victory or bust party on election night. He hoped she wasn't still steamed about the judge granting the temporary settlement orders Joe had submitted, giving his client the advantage.

If he lost this election, and she stayed to commiserate with him, he'd know she was more than a little interested in him. To his surprise, she said yes, she'd be there and cheer for him.

She didn't sound like she was still steamed at him. And he liked that she cared about him winning. That was good too.

Two days later, soon after seven when the polls closed, he paced before the table with a cake decorated only with his name. If he had them write Congratulations on it, that might jinx things. The punch bowl smelled of peach ice cream and fizzled, probably full of 7 Up or something similar. Not knowing who'd show up, he'd vetoed something stronger.

His assistant had taped his banner saying "Morales for Legislature" on the wall behind the table. A crowd of his friends stood around talking, but there were also people he'd seen at his town hall meetings. That encouraged him, but would enough people vote for him, or would that damn Cash Carter win?

He paced the floor as a large-screen TV kept reporting on the tallies. When the announcer stated he was ahead, everyone clapped and yelled, then quieted down to watch the progress. He crossed his fingers.

Kayla approached him. "It's looking good. I hope you win."

He grinned. "Thanks. I'm glad you came, but it's too soon to tell anything."

More reports came in from the precincts. First Carter was ahead, then Joe was. Kayla pointed to Carter's name. "I bet he was behind your slashed tires. Did your insurance company pay to fix them?"

"They did. I'm sure you're right about Cash being behind it. Wish I could prove it. I'd hate to have him making the laws for our state."

Someone shouted, "Morales is ahead." Afraid to hope, Joe looked. He was, but only by fifty votes. That could change any moment. An announcer said that ninety-three percent of the precincts had reported. Joe glanced at Kayla. She had crossed fingers on both hands. That made him smile. She'd be a loyal supporter, a woman who'd stand by his side.

The count went to one hundred above Carter, then

two hundred eighty, with ninety-eight percent of the votes tallied. Then the announcer said, "I'm calling this one for Joe Morales, our next representative for the legislature."

Everyone clapped and cheered. Joe could hardly believe he'd won. His campaign manager shook Joe's hand. He was riding high now. Kayla hugged him. "You made it. You made it," she said.

Being hugged by her felt good. She smelled like gardenias.

Laughter and cheers filled the room. His heart felt so light, he might even float up to the ceiling.

"Where's a knife?" Kayla asked. "You need to cut your victory cake now."

He cut the first piece, set it on a paper plate, and handed it to her. "Ladies first."

She handed it to him. "You're the victory man. This is for you. I'll cut my own." However, she stood there and served all the crowd before taking one for herself.

Joe couldn't help but smile as he said thank you to all the visitors. After they ate cake, congratulated him, and filed out, his campaign manager said, "I'll clean up if you want to leave now." He glanced at Kayla. "I sure wouldn't want to hang around here if I had a lovely lady like her by my side."

"Thanks, Bill, I'd appreciate that. Kayla, may I follow you home? I don't trust Carter to accept my election without causing trouble. I'd hate for him to try something with you, just in case he's seen us together."

"That's not necessary," Kayla said. "I've been reluctant to mention it, but I used to date Cash Carter. I broke up with him, but I don't think he'd try to hurt me just to get back at you."

That threw Joe for a loop. His heart beat erratically. How could she have put up with that obnoxious clown? "Nevertheless, it's late, and I'd feel better if I see you home."

"Thanks. I appreciate that." As they walked toward the door, she said in low tones, "I drove, but you can follow me home and come in for coffee if you'd like. Guess I shouldn't have made such a stink after the judge's ruling in the *Witherspoon* case. I know you were only trying to get the best deal for your client."

She picked up her jacket from a chair near the door. He took hold of it. "Let me help you with that." Standing behind her, he liked her fresh scent as she slipped into it. That brought back memories of her body touching his. He smiled. That night had been wonderful beyond his expectations.

"Thanks," she said as they walked out into the cool November air. He took her hand. He still felt a little tingle when he took hold of it. She smiled at him and squeezed his hand. Anyone who saw them like this might think they weren't doing as much as possible for their respective clients, but right now, he didn't care.

He hoped to hell no one took a picture of them walking together like this. The judge might throw out their divorce case and insist each party get a new attorney. Reluctantly, he let go of her hand. He wanted to put an arm around her shoulders but thought better of it. "It's nice to have you on my team."

She smiled. "I'm glad you have lots of others."

He walked to her car, then headed for his. After waiting until he heard her start the engine, he followed her home, still feeling exalted about winning the election.

He parked on the street while she pulled into a covered parking spot. He got out and joined her as she walked toward the building door. She patted his shoulder, and he caught another whiff of gardenias.

"I knew you'd win. You're a better man than Cash Carter."

"You're smarter than he is and much prettier."

She smiled. "Thanks."

****

At the entrance to her building, Kayla pushed in the security code numbers on a keypad and held the door open for him. His sandalwood aftershave washed over her. He sure smelled good. He followed her up the steps and along the hallway to her apartment door. She was about to unlock it when she heard a noise. It sounded like something falling on the floor. Joe grabbed her arm. "Wait. You don't have a pet, do you?"

"No. But I'm not sure if that noise came from my apartment or the one next door."

She stood listening for a few minutes and heard a thump.

Sure now, that those noises must come from her place, she trembled. Bats flew around inside her stomach. She was glad she wasn't alone. "Should I call the cops?"

"We don't have any actual evidence to tell them," Joe said. He put his ear to the door. "I don't hear anything now. Hand me your key. I'm going in."

"But what if someone is in there and attacks you?"

He frowned. "I can take care of myself. Just stand back."

She pulled out her phone to call the police as he unlocked the door and barged in.

Clutching a bulging pillowcase against his chest, a big, burly man shoved Joe back against Kayla. She struggled to keep her balance and screamed. "Help. Help. Someone's attacking us."

Doors down the hall opened. Neighbors peeked out. The thief brushed past Kayla. Nearly knocked her over. He ran down the stairs. Joe chased after him. She dialed 911. Tried to get a good look at him.

The dispatcher asked for her name and address. Then he asked what had happened. Kayla told him as much as she could.

Joe hurried back up the steps, panting. "I can't believe he got away."

She held out the phone. "Here, talk to the dispatcher."

Joe took the phone. "The guy was about six feet tall. He must weigh about 260." Joe handed the phone back to her.

Still holding the phone to her ear, she walked back into her apartment. "The dispatcher wants us both to wait for the police. You might as well come in and sit down while we wait." Thank goodness Joe had gone in first. She touched his arm. It felt firm and well-muscled. He could have protected her from the burglar. "That guy was pretty rough. Did he hurt you?"

"No. He just startled me. Are you okay?"

"I'm fine. But we'd better not touch anything that might have fingerprints." She scanned her living room and gasped. Her red pillows lay on the floor beside her couch. The landscape picture hung crooked over her gray couch.

Dreading what she'd find, she peeked in her bedroom. Her jewelry box lay open, a long necklace

65

dangling from it as if too cheap to bother with. Good thing her taste ran to good-looking costume jewelry instead of diamonds and emeralds, but no jewelry seemed to be missing. Her bed was mussed, and her pillow lay on the floor minus the pillowcase.

A few papers from her desk lay on the floor, but her computer looked untouched. Was this a random burglary, or was he after something specific—but what could it be? A sinking feeling welled up inside. Where were the two fat files of research she'd downloaded from the Internet and brought home to study?

She hurried back into the living room. Her coffee table was bare. "I'm missing two file folders of research on sinkholes. Damn it, I'll have to redo it."

She glanced at Joe. Would he go so far as to hire someone to steal her research? She didn't know him that well, but one thing stood out. He was very ambitious when it came to winning cases. "I'll need more time to redo all that research, organize it, and get ready for trial. Would you agree to postponing the court date?"

"With the court backed up the way it is, it may be weeks before we can get another date. Are you sure you want to delay the case that long? I thought your client wanted to get paid for fixing up his property sooner rather than later."

She stared at Joe. He sounded reasonable, but he seemed eager to keep the court date only a little more than a week away. "You sure you had nothing to do with this? If you use any evidence from my folders which I haven't provided to you already as required by discovery rules, I'll report you to the Texas bar and charge you with using fruit from a poisonous tree."

His eyebrows angled closer together, and his chin

jutted out. "Some thanks I get for chasing a burglar away. Believe me, I had nothing to do with this break-in." He glared at her. "How could you believe I'd do something so underhanded? I'll win the case fair and square. My client's not at fault for a freak accident caused by nature."

"I'm not sure what to think. You'd better go."

"Well, I'll see you in court. And yes, I'll agree to a postponement so you can redo your damn research." He turned and strode toward the door. "I'm leaving."

"Wait. You need to stay until the police come."

"Okay, fine." He frowned. "I'll wait, but I'm not staying here with you any minute longer."

His blunt statement grated on her nerves. She probably shouldn't have been so quick to accuse him.

A little while later, when two police officers came, neither Joe nor she could add much to the description of the burglar they'd given earlier. The police didn't stay long. Joe left as a fingerprint expert dusted her coffee table and the doorknob with black powder. He took pictures, then left.

Finally, her apartment was quiet. Free from the sound of Joe's voice—free from sandalwood scent—and damn it, free from the touch of his arms around her. True, she'd told him their wonderful evening together was a mistake, but she'd thought they had the beginning of a relationship—something they could explore once their two cases were over. *Never had she been drawn so strongly to a man, but now she felt scorned and empty.*

Enough dwelling on Joe. She needed to replace her research. She couldn't wait for the paralegal she shared with Laura to do it.

Trying to stop thinking about Joe, she sat at her

computer on the desk in her bedroom and Googled sinkholes in Texas again. She'd have to furnish all the material she was presenting at court as evidence before the trial, so she needed to print copies.

Soon, her printer buzzed and spit out papers filled with print and pictures. She studied pictures of core samples, wishing she'd taken a course in geology. If Richard Black ever produced a core sample from Thad Thayer's property, she'd have to call the geologist she'd hired to analyze a core soil sample from her client's backyard.

Damn it, why would anyone but Joe or Richard Black feel the need to steal her research material? He could have asked for copies using a request for production. She smothered a yawn. It had been a long night. She couldn't focus. Time to go to bed.

But after taking a shower, she couldn't stop thinking about Joe. How good it felt to hug him at the victory party. He'd been so excited to win, and she was glad for him, but was his client behind the burglary?

Finally, after tossing and turning, she drifted off to sleep.

In the morning, she called her client Thad Thayer in to question him about when he saw the sinkhole starting. Tall and slim, he sat in her office, ran his hands through his auburn hair, and brushed his mustache. "I first noticed it the first of this month with a small hole in my backyard. Now it's two yards across."

Kayla wrote the date.

"Can you imagine how scary it is to watch more dirt keep falling from the sides of the sinkhole every day? The door on the back of my screened-in porch is hard to open because the floor is sinking. I shoveled dirt under the edges, but that didn't help."

She was writing all he said when her father called.

"Dad, I have a client here. Can you call later?"

"I'll just take a minute. The legislature isn't meeting in Austin until Friday, and I don't need to leave until tomorrow morning. Would you like to join me for lunch today? I invited your brother to join us, but he wrecked his car and can't come."

"You mean the car you gave him half the down payment for?" Kayla frowned. Dad had never offered to do that for her. "He can walk to classes and get a job to pay for fixing it."

"That's what I told him. Where do you want to eat?"

"The Red Skillet."

"I love the food at the Red Skillet."

Thad, her client, leaned forward. "That's a great place. Remember, I'm assistant manager there."

"By the way," her father said, "Joe Morales will join us. I understand you're involved in one or two of his cases. Will that be a problem?"

What should she tell him—that she didn't want to be sharing a table with him—that he did his best to cheat a poor woman out of needed training and maybe had stolen her research to delay her? "Sorry, Dad, I've got a client here I need to confer with, and it might take a while. I'd better beg off. Maybe next time you're in town. Talk to you later." She disconnected.

"Hey," Thad Thayer said. "Don't worry about me. I have to get back to work."

"You must get paid well as an assistant manager to afford a house in that development."

"I made a large down payment, so the bank

approved the loan. Now I have to finance the payment to the contractor who's going to fill in the sinkhole. If you win my case soon, I can afford to pay him in full for getting the hole filled and my house shored up."

As Thad hurried out, she wondered what Joe would say about her to her father. If asked about Joe, she could unleash a mouthful, how he'd acted like he was attracted to her, kept leading her on, and then might have encouraged his client to steal her research.

****

An hour later, Joe entered the Red Skillet. Pictures of cowboys leading herds decorated the walls, and the smell of beef cooking filled the air. David Walker sat at a table in the corner. Joe walked over, shook hands, and sat down. Soon a pleasant-faced waitress took their orders for pulled pork sandwiches with potato salad.

Over the chatter of conversation in the restaurant, David said, "The Land and Resources Management Committee recommended we pass the bill to expand the area for Cedar Hill State Park. I've scheduled debate on it for Thursday morning and scheduled a vote on it for that afternoon. We've spent enough time on it, and it's time we deal with other pressing matters. I'd like you to get sworn in as soon as possible so you can be present to vote on it."

As Joe leaned back in his chair, a male employee washed a table in a booth across from their table, straightened the salt and pepper shakers, and took a long time wiping down the seats.

"I can't wait to take my seat," Joe said. "My constituents would welcome more room for family picnics. As I told a reporter last week, I plan to vote for the park extension."

David sipped his drink. "I invited Kayla to join us, but she declined. From what I can tell, she's doing a real good job."

Joe took a deep breath. He hated being attracted to an attorney who would face him in court, but he felt bad she didn't trust him after someone broke into her place.

After the court hearing for the divorce case when the judge granted his client's requests for the temporary orders, she'd given him an earful. If Joe got the husband what he wanted in the divorce and won the sinkhole case for his client, Richard Black, would she still refuse to go out with him? He hoped not. He really liked her and would like to continue a relationship with her after their two cases were settled.

Finally, their food arrived, and both men tucked in.

After they finished, Joe said, "Let's have some pie. I saw some chocolate pie in the display case."

Her father laughed. "Kayla likes anything chocolate. I always give her a box of candy at her birthday dinner. Kayla offers everyone in the family a piece and then quickly shuts the box and takes it home after dinner." He waved the waitress over. Joe ordered lemon, and David asked for pecan.

As they finished, they talked for a while over coffee about the legislative bills coming up. Joe leaned forward. "Texas should increase the amount the state pays for education. We need to stop that so-called 'Robin Hood' law that requires the richer school districts to give up some of their taxes to help poorer districts. If people are willing to pay to enrich education in their district, the school district should receive the benefits, and the state should take care of the poorer districts."

David nodded. "A couple of representatives have

already filed bills to finally repeal that law." He looked at his watch. "It's two o'clock. I'd better go." He picked up the check. "I won't wish you good luck on your case with Kayla, because I want her to win."

Joe laughed. "You're prejudiced, but I hope my father feels the same way about me." Hell, he didn't know how his father felt about Joe's work. Would his father even recognize him as the dementia progressed further?

As they walked out to their cars, a pain developed in Joe's stomach. He was also nauseous. "I don't feel so good. The potato salad tasted off."

David's face looked pale. "Isn't it too soon for food poisoning?" He clutched his stomach. "But I'm feeling bad also."

Joe turned back toward the Red Skillet. "I should try to retrieve what's left on our plates."

Chapter Six

Trying to hold the nausea at bay, Joe rushed back in the restaurant. A busboy was carrying a large basin loaded with plates. "Stop. I want to see the plate I left on that table." He pointed to where they'd sat.

The busboy shook his head. "Those dishes are already in the dishwasher."

Disappointed, Joe went back outside. David was vomiting in the bushes and holding his stomach. Joe tasted sour liquid and spat into the bushes. Now his stomach hurt really bad. "We need to go to the emergency room."

David coughed up more vomit and mumbled, "You're probably right. Call a taxi? Don't think I can drive."

Joe yanked a handkerchief from his pocket. "Come on to my car." Surely, he could manage to get them there. Besides, the leather seats were washable.

Taking David's arm, Joe led him to his car. David walked with halting steps, groaning most of the way. Joe settled David in the passenger seat. Trying to stem his own nausea, Joe drove to Parkland Hospital and parked near the emergency room. After spitting out a mouthful of foul liquid, he managed to get David to the door of the emergency room, where an attendant met them. "Our stomachs hurt, and we're nauseated, both of us," was all he could get out before clutching his own stomach.

"Hurts like hell."

Later, after giving out basic information, they sat on uncomfortable chairs in a small waiting room. Joe heard the clerk calling the Red Skillet and asking if anyone else got sick. From her response, he gathered he and David were the only ones. The smell of disinfectant and coffee brewing lingered in the air and intensified Joe's nausea. Glare from the sun shot through the window, making him blink. His pain throbbed. David was moaning.

David fumbled in his pocket and pulled out his phone. "Need to call my wife. Can't seem to focus on my contact list."

Joe held up his phone. "I'll call Kayla. I've got her number."

Now he, too, had a hard time focusing on her name. Luckily, he managed to get it right the first time. It rang and rang. Why wasn't she picking up? Must be still mad at him. He left a message. "Kayla, call me. Your father and I are at the ER. Think it's food poisoning. He's in bad shape."

Joe ran his fingers through his hair and waited. Within seconds, his phone rang.

"Where are you?"

"Parkland, at the emergency room."

"I'll be there as soon as I can."

He was glad Kayla was coming, but he must look and smell awful. If she still blamed him for the break-in, would she even care? After he hung up, he turned to David. "You know, they might want to keep us overnight."

David frowned. "Damn it. I need to call the speaker pro tem to reschedule the vote. I have great confidence in him, but he is against the bill to extend the park and may call the vote, hoping it won't pass."

David grabbed his phone, rubbed his eyes, and pushed a button. "Hey, Burton, I'm in the emergency room…think it's food poisoning. Joe Morales, the new rep from Dallas, is sick, too. Can't make it tomorrow. Reschedule the vote on the park extension bill. Set it for the following Friday." He listened for a moment, rubbing his stomach. "Damn it, Burton, don't get drunk on power. You shouldn't schedule a vote when several reps are missing."

David listened for a moment, then heaved a sigh of relief. "Thanks. I appreciate it, and so does Joe."

"Did he postpone the vote?" Joe asked.

David nodded.

"That's good. I didn't want to miss the first vote after being elected."

An attendant in blue scrubs came to take Joe to an examining room. Once there, she took his blood pressure and checked his pulse.

A doctor checked him and asked questions about his severe pain. "It may be more serious than food poisoning. First, you need to have your stomach pumped."

Through the door, he saw Kayla come rushing to see her father. He hoped David didn't feel as bad.

Twenty minutes later, Kayla walked into Joe's room. The concern on her face was welcome, but he couldn't tell if it was just for her father or for both of them. She glanced at Joe and frowned. "My dad's not feeling well. How are you doing?"

Joe placed his hands on his abdomen. "Not much better," Joe admitted. "I probably feel worse."

"I'm sorry. What does the doctor say?"

"They're sending me to get my stomach pumped, and they might want your father to, also. By the way, David said you were doing a good job as a new attorney."

"Thanks for telling me that. It's nice to hear my dad compliment me." She smiled and stood up straighter.

Joe clutched the sides of his abdomen again and groaned.

"You feeling really bad now?"

"It hurts a little, but I'm okay. The nurse said they will schedule me for an MRI to check for appendicitis."

"Oh, no. I hope it's not that. Can I bring you anything? Would you like some flowers?"

Joe shook his head. "Those are nice for you women, but I don't care for them."

"I know. I'll bring books. Dad likes murder mysteries. What do you like, Joe?"

Joe opened his eyes wide. That was pretty nice of her, especially after he had won the case against her client. "I haven't read the latest book by David Baldacci, but I hate for you to go to any trouble."

"Since I'm going to visit Barnes and Noble for a mystery for Dad, I'll buy it for you, but only if I read it first." She laughed. "Guess that would defeat the purpose, because you'll be out of here by then."

Did she still think he was behind the burglary? Might as well ask. "Kayla, do you really think I'd have someone break into your place?"

She looked at him, then shook her head. "I guess you wouldn't be that unprofessional."

"Thanks for the vote of confidence."

"However, given the stolen files concerned your client's case, I wonder if he had something to do with it."

Joe frowned. "Don't accuse him unless you have

proof."

Her determined chin jutted out. "I'll ask the police if the fingerprints from my place match any on file for your client."

Hoping his client hadn't stolen them, he could foresee heated arguments in court. "Hey, I'm going to win this case fair and square. Never mind getting a book. I'll see you in court."

****

As Kayla strode from the examining room, the odor of bleach mingled with that of brewing coffee. Joe's powerful arms contrasted with his pale face as he lay there. He was so enticing when he was being nice. Here she was trying to do him a favor, and he had to go and spoil it all.

She hoped he'd get well soon, but regardless of being attracted, she'd stay away from him as much as possible.

His client probably was behind the break-in. Why would anyone else want those files? Was Joe friends with that judge who ruled on the temporary orders in favor of Joe's client and denied her client the expense money she needed? Joe was a professional. She had to stop thinking like that until she knew the facts.

After stopping at a nearby Barnes and Noble, she bought a mystery for Dad. Oh, well, why not get David Baldacci's latest book? Surely, no one could accuse them of colluding on a case because she loaned him a book.

When she returned to his room, she held out the book. "I bought the book for myself, but I'll lend it to you while you're laid up. When you're through, I can pick it up from your office."

He smiled. "After I snapped at you, that's really nice

of you. I'm almost embarrassed to take it, but I love Baldacci's books, so I'll take it and give it back after I read it. Thanks a lot."

She placed the book in his hand and noticed the slight tingle. Damn. Touching him still affected her. She really should resist that. "Uh, you're welcome. Don't hurry to finish it. I have plenty of work to keep me busy."

He smiled again. "You should take time out to play sometimes."

His eyes twinkled, making her want to ask if he had anything in mind, but no matter how interesting that sounded, hanging out with him was unprofessional. "I will, one of these days, but now I need to check on Dad and get back to work. Enjoy the read. I'll see you later." She walked out quickly before he could say anything else.

****

Joe glanced past a nurse taking his blood pressure to see Ellen, his former girlfriend, standing in the doorway, dressed in a tight, red sweater that showed off her boobs. She held a book in her hand. "How are you feeling?"

"Really nauseous. I may have food poisoning."

She held out a book. "I brought you *The Fallen,* a David Baldacci novel."

It looked new, and he didn't want to hurt her feelings, but maybe she could return it. "That was thoughtful of you, but I've already read that one."

"Oh well, I can take it back. But what I really came to tell you is I have two tickets for a concert with John Legend. I know you like his songs."

Joe groaned. His stomach hurt so much he could hardly come up with a polite refusal. "Really, Ellen, I'm in the hospital, and you want to have this conversation again? I thought I made that clear the last time we talked. I'd just want to hang out with other people."

"But we were so good together. What's changed? Have you met someone else?"

"Being with you is too much like living with my mother. You tell me I should wear a sweater when it's only a little chilly."

"You mean I'm bossy?"

This discussion made his stomach even more unsettled. He wished she'd leave. "Well, yes."

"I'm the oldest in my family, and I used to take care of my younger siblings. It's sort of a habit, but what if I try not to act like that anymore? I really want to get back together."

Joe sighed. His belly hurt a lot. "I'm not asking you to change for me. Why don't you find another man who enjoys being with you?"

Ellen frowned. "That woman I just saw leaving your room—is she your new girlfriend?"

He shook his head, then wished he hadn't as a new wave of nausea hit him. He fished for a handkerchief in his pocket. "She's the opposing attorney in two of my cases, but it's her father who ate lunch with me, and we both got food poisoning." He held the handkerchief to his mouth. "I might be sick again. Please leave." Was he going to throw up right in front of her? He groaned. It wouldn't be nice to imply she made him sick.

Ellen left, and Joe barely made it to the bathroom. After vomiting, he rinsed his mouth and felt better. He crawled back in bed, pulled up the covers, and lay down to rest until they pumped his stomach.

Quick footsteps and a gravelly voice calling his name aroused him. Joe turned over and opened his eyes.

"Hey, Representative Morales, wake up. I've got something for you," the man said. A hoodie shaded his face, leaving only his dark, shaggy beard threaded with gray hairs visible.

"Who are you, and why are you in my room?"

With gloved fingers, the man slapped a nine-by-twelve envelope on Joe's chest and walked out.

Joe pushed the button for the nurse. A woman's voice came over the speaker. "May we help you? What do you need?"

"An unidentified man walked into my room and left an envelope. Would you please call security?"

"Don't touch the envelope. Someone from security will come check on it."

Joe groaned. "My stomach really hurts. Can someone please check on me?"

"A nurse will be there shortly. And I'll ask the security officer to come."

Joe lay still, his chin propped on his chest, staring at the envelope. Surely, a paper envelope wouldn't explode, but there might be anthrax or something worse inside.

After what seemed like an eternity, a uniformed man knocked on the door.

"Come in," Joe said. "And please take this envelope off my chest."

"Did someone put that on top of you?"

Joe nodded. "Some man I didn't know. He left in a hurry. Did anyone try to stop him before he left?"

"One of the nurses called about that, but we didn't find any unauthorized persons in the hospital."

"Well, please take it away. I don't know what's in it, but I want it off my chest."

After donning gloves, the security officer snatched the envelope. While Joe waited, he turned it over, undid the string around the clasp, lifted the flap, and peered inside.

"Nothing in here but a piece of paper."

"Would you take it out and see what it says?"

Holding the corner edge with his finger and thumb, the security officer pulled it out. Bold dark letters showed through the back of the paper.

"What does it say?" Joe asked.

" 'Vote for park enlargement, and you'll be sorry.' "

"Is there a signature?"

The security officer shook his head. "That's all it says. Sounds like a threat."

"Would you please call the police and ask them to check it for fingerprints," Joe said.

As he left, a nurse walked in with a wheelchair. "I'm taking you to get your stomach pumped now." He got out of bed and sat in the chair as she wheeled him down the hall. He'd beaten Cash Carter in the election, but the would-be representative might be up to some dirty work.

Joe scratched his head. Or maybe someone else was.

Chapter Seven

After getting coffee from the cafeteria, Kayla passed the doorway of Joe's hospital room. Lit up by sunshine coming in the window, a young woman stood facing Joe. Wearing a tight-fitting sweater and a short skirt, she obviously wasn't a nurse.

A male nurse walked by, pausing a moment to glance at the woman. She had a pretty face and long, blonde curly hair like Kayla's younger sister, Denice, who always had plenty of young men calling on the phone or taking her on dates.

That reminded Kayla of her mother's comments. "Your hair may not be blonde, but you could at least curl it." At least Mom hadn't said Denice was prettier than Kayla. Even now, the memories of her mother's favoritism for Denice reared up. And Mom still mentioned she'd like Kayla to find some nice guy and get married.

Well, Kayla had her own agenda. She wanted to win cases and impress the other attorneys at her firm, especially the managing partner. Maybe after working there for six or seven years, someday, she'd manage to be accepted as an equity partner.

She glanced again at Joe. He seemed to be in deep discussion with that woman, obviously someone he knew well. Frowning, Kayla walked by without saying hello or waving at him. Seeing that woman did nothing to stop the way Kayla felt about Joe—although it should have. They didn't need to be attracted to each other while they were on different sides of not one, but two cases.

She shoved that attraction deep down and tried to ignore it. That shouldn't bother her, but it did. Footsteps of nurses hurrying by with squeaky carts echoed against the walls. As she stepped in her father's room, the smell of disinfectant hovered in the air. "How are you feeling now?"

"A little better after throwing up all my lunch. They said they'd release me if I don't get worse in a couple of hours."

"I'll sit and talk with you if you feel up to it."

"I'd like that. Thanks again for the mystery book." He talked about the difficulty of getting representatives from opposite sides to pass bills that were needed to take care of things in the state.

She told him she'd found arguing in court was stressful, even though she had prepared her talking points. "I not only concentrate on what to say, I watch the jurors' faces. I want to see if they understood and might agree with my side."

Later, after talking awhile with her dad, she walked into Joe's room. "Hi. You're looking better. My dad's being dismissed. I hope the MRI doesn't show you have appendicitis."

Joe shook his head. "They found isopropyl alcohol in my stomach. Somebody at the Red Skillet must have poisoned our food."

"Oh, no. Who would do that? Did you call the police and ask them to investigate?"

"I sure did, but we'll have to wait and see what they find out."

Still annoyed at seeing that other woman in his room, Kayla debated about mentioning her. Why not ask? That would be smarter than wondering. "I wouldn't have bothered to bring you a book if I'd known you had someone to keep you company."

"Ellen's an old girlfriend. She called my office and found out I was here. She came to see me because she had some tickets for a John Legend concert, and asked me to go with her. I told her I wasn't interested."

"I see." He'd said he wasn't interested, and Kayla felt somewhat relieved. However, that woman probably hadn't given up on Joe. Kayla wanted to see more of him as soon as their opposing cases were over. For now, they needed to keep their relationship strictly business, and she had work to do. She headed toward the door.

"Wait a minute, Kayla. I need to tell you something."

Frowning, she turned to face him. "What is it?"

His eyebrows came closer together. "I got a threatening note warning me not to vote for the park extension bill. Would you have any idea who might have sent it?"

"What?" Kayla asked, walking back toward Joe's hospital bed. "Why would you think I might?"

"The note said if I voted for the park extension, I'd be sorry. Your client's property ends next to that area. Maybe he's got something hidden he doesn't want people to see in those woods."

She frowned. "Why blame my client?"

"He's accusing Richard Black of being responsible for the sinkhole. Your client probably resents because I'm his lawyer."

Kayla shook her head. "As far as I know, Thad

Thayer has nothing to do with your threatening note. Your client is a developer. He might want to use that land. What about the break-in at my place? Have you asked Richard Black if he arranged that? I spent hours redoing that research. I need to see my father. I'll see you in court."

Her stomach churned. She couldn't leave the room fast enough. Why was she so attracted to him? For all she knew, his good looks might cover a troublesome personality. It was foolish to assume he'd really be interested in her, a forceful career attorney. Besides, she had more important things to think about. She needed to help her father get ready to go home, and stop thinking about Joe Morales, the bastard.

Still seething, she walked back to her father's room. "Are you ready to leave?"

"If you'll wait outside so I can get dressed, I'll let you know when I'm ready."

She paced in the hall, taking a few minutes to cool down. How could Joe have been so nice and appealing when he talked to her earlier, then assume the worst about her client?

When her father called, "Come in now," she opened the door. He sat on the bed, fully dressed. His face looked pale, but he was signing a paper on a clipboard, probably the release.

A middle-aged nurse walked in, pushing a wheelchair.

Her father shook his head. "I'm fine. I don't need a wheelchair. Kayla, if you'd drive me home, I'd appreciate it. I called your mother, but I told her not to worry because I'm feeling better." Looking a bit unsteady on his feet, he rose. Kayla hurried to take his arm as he shuffled toward the doorway.

The nurse pointed to the wheelchair. "Sorry, sir. Hospital orders. I have to wheel you to the car." She glanced at Kayla. "You could drive your car around to the front door, and I'll bring him out."

Her father frowned but walked over and plopped down in the wheelchair. Kayla took the plastic bag with his stuff and hurried out to bring her car to the front door.

Later, when she pulled up next to the sidewalk, the nurse helped her father get into the passenger seat. As Kayla drove away, her father said, "Thanks for taking me home. Are they releasing Joe too?"

Kayla shook her head. "They want to keep him longer and do an MRI to be sure he doesn't have appendicitis."

"I've been mentoring him, and now I'm proud to see he's matured into an excellent attorney. He's a nice young man. You could do well with him."

She shook her head. "Dad, I can't date him." If he was as nice as he'd been earlier, it might have been fun to go dancing with him, but tight-sweater gal might win him back. "He's on the opposite side of not one, but two of my cases. I'd really like to beat him in both."

"You're a good lawyer, and you're smart. If you have a strong case, I'm sure you'll come out ahead."

"Thanks for the vote of confidence."

Her father leaned back and closed his eyes. Kayla hoped he was just tired and not still feeling sick as she drove toward his home.

Her mother met them at the door with a worried face and helped her father walk down the hall to the bedroom. Kayla followed and stood in the doorway while her mother bustled around, removing her father's suit jacket and shoes. "Just lie there and nap. I'll fix Kayla some coffee."

As they headed for the kitchen, Kayla was glad her parents were still together and still loved each other. Would she be lucky enough to marry someone she loved and be as happy as her parents were?

Seated at the kitchen table, she sipped coffee from a red mug. Outside, a cardinal sat on a branch close to the window. "I'm sure Dad will be all right soon."

Her mother sat down across from her. "I've eaten there many times and never got ill. Maybe they used some ingredient they'd kept around too long."

Kayla shook her head. "The food was poisoned."

"Poisoned? What do you mean?"

"The man Dad was eating lunch with said they found rubbing alcohol in his stomach. Dad probably got some also. We need to sue the restaurant."

"That's awful. Thanks for bringing him home from the hospital. I guess I've been a bit critical of you in the past, but…" Her mother reached over and touched her hand. "I want you to know I'm proud of what you've accomplished. It isn't every woman who can go head-to-head with experienced attorneys in court."

Warm feelings filled Kayla's chest. What a pleasant surprise. "Thanks, Mom. It's good to hear that."

"How do you like working at that big firm?"

"I have to share a paralegal with another attorney, and as low man, I mean woman, on the totem pole, I don't get the bigger cases."

"That's too bad."

"I've applied at other firms, but so far, no one's interested."

"Well, maybe if you win the sinkhole case, other

firms will take notice."

"I only got the sinkhole one because Thad was my neighbor and asked me to take his case."

"Well, I hope you win. No one should lose their house to a sinkhole."

Kayla sipped her coffee. "I have plenty of evidence, and I think I have a good chance of winning."

Her mother smiled. "I'm sure you will."

Kayla finished her coffee. "I've got to get back to work. I'll see you later." She hugged her mother and left.

When she got to her office, Beth said, "There's a message for you."

"Who is it from?" Kayla asked.

"Joe Morales."

"I'll listen, but I don't have time to call him back now."

Her legal assistant pushed the message button.

Joe's deep voice came from the speaker. "I don't have appendicitis. They're letting me head back to my office now. Thanks again for the book. I'll enjoy reading it. I'm looking forward to seeing you again so I can give it back."

He spoke like he was still interested in seeing her. Kayla gripped the edge of her desk and stared at the phone. Was Joe the kind of man, like Clay, or rather Cash as he was known now, who would charm several women at the same time? Joe had said Ellen was an ex-girlfriend, but he could have other women he hung out with.

Kayla fisted her hands. She didn't need him. She was an accomplished attorney, someone who mattered to Rose and Thad. She could help them get justice. That's why she became a lawyer.

She should forget about the night she and Joe gave

in to impulse, except that night kept glowing like a shining star in her mind. She wished they could be together like that again. Wouldn't that be heaven?

She sighed. Oh well, she needed to get busy drafting interrogatory questions the attorney for the other side was required to answer about his client's case. She'd also draft a request for production to get copies of documents from Joe's client regarding her client's property. That way she wouldn't encounter any big surprises during trial.

Beth said, "Thad Thayer is on the phone."

After she greeted him, Thad said, "I think the sinkhole is getting closer to my house."

"Why don't you measure it and call me back?"

A few minutes later, Thad phoned. "It's a foot and a half closer than it was a week ago. I'm worried. I need to get it fixed, but I will have a hard time paying for it before my case is settled. Would you please come out and photograph it to use for evidence?"

"I'll be there shortly."

After she ended the call, she rang Joe. "My client's sinkhole is getting larger. It's a foot and a half closer to his house than last week."

"He must be exaggerating."

"I don't think so. I'm going out to take pictures. If you don't believe that, come and see for yourself."

"I've got a lot of work here. I don't think I can fit it into my schedule."

"Suit yourself, but you should see how big it is and how close it is to his house. Consider persuading your client to agree to our demand before it gets bigger and my client wants more money."

"Go on out and take pictures, but I don't think he'll

settle."

Fifteen minutes later, she parked in front of the house. Small shrubs surrounded the one-story yellow brick house. The smell of cut grass wafted by.

Thad met her at the door. She caught the faint odor of pot. He held a yardstick in his hand. "Come out back, and I'll show you."

She followed him around to the back of the house. A low stone wall enclosed a flagstone-covered patio. A couple of terra-cotta pots of red geraniums sat in the corners.

"This looks nice. Did the patio come with the house?"

Thad shook his head. "I put it in. Took a lot of work. I sure don't want to lose it all to that damn sinkhole."

Outside the low wall surrounding the patio, a patch of mint waving in a gentle breeze filled the air with a pleasant tang.

Thad pointed to a green plastic chair. "Have a seat." As she sat, he perched on another chair. "I've gotten estimates on filling this. I hope you can get my case settled before it gets any worse."

"The trial should happen soon."

"By the way, has Joe Morales said anything about voting for the park extension? I don't want that passed. That area needs to stay in reserve for the wildlife so bobcats and coyotes don't move into our neighborhoods.

"Besides," Thad added, "my neighbors and I don't want our homes overrun with rats the leftover food from picnickers will attract."

"I hardly think it will come to that. Since Morales is the representative from your district, why don't you write him a letter?"

"I already sent him a note, but I thought you might know which way he leans."

"We only talk about the two cases we have together." Except they'd done more than talking that night. She could still remember his hands touching her skin. And how wonderful she'd felt afterward. She sighed. Too bad he was forbidden territory.

"Did he mention that he'd received a note from me?" Thad asked.

"Was that the one that said if he voted for the park extension, he'd be sorry?"

"I don't remember exactly what I wrote," Thad said.

"Mr. Morales got a threatening note. If you wrote that one, you could be arrested."

"Richard Black, the developer, could have sent it. He probably wants to build on that land." Thad looked worried. "Do you think the other attorney will try to press charges against someone? I didn't write I was going to shoot him or come at him with a knife. Besides, you can't talk to him about that. Attorney–client privilege."

"No, I won't, but as your attorney, I'd advise you not to do or say anything else that might get you in trouble."

Thad frowned. "If he blames me, will that hurt my case?"

"It sure won't help us get a favorable settlement."

"Damn." He glanced at the sinkhole. "I need something done fast, or I might lose my house and everything in it." He waved his arm over his yard. "And my landscaping, too."

Giving the hole a wide berth, Kayla stepped closer to the edge of his yard. Bushes that appeared to be marijuana extended into the wooded area. Was he growing that for his own use, or was he planning to sell some? She didn't want to know.

Her client laid a yardstick next to the flagstone patio and started measuring the distance. She took a few pictures of the hole. It must be eight feet in diameter. A clump of dirt on the edge tumbled loose and fell into it. She couldn't see the bottom from where she stood.

Thad kept flipping the yardstick as he measured.

The grass closer to the sinkhole appeared yellower than the rest. The sinkhole must be drawing water away from the soil. Maybe there would be water in the bottom of the hole. Holding her camera, she stepped closer to see.

She stuck her heels in the dirt to anchor herself as she leaned over to take another shot. She guessed the hole was ten feet deep. And, yes, there was water in the bottom. She aimed the camera to get a good picture.

The soil gave way beneath her. She tossed her camera onto the soft grass behind her. "Help!"

She stuck out her arms. Reached out to grasp something. Anything. Grabbed dry grass. It broke in her fingers.

And she kept sliding. Down. Sticking out her arms to the side, she grasped at the dirt. That didn't slow her fall. Stones and dry lumps of dirt raked her back as she fell. Her hair caught on something, pulling at her scalp. Then it loosened. Whatever it was must have broken off some hair.

"Stick out your hand," Thad yelled.

Turning her head, she looked up. Thad's face appeared at the edge of the hole. Dirt fell in her eyes. She could barely see him.

She brushed her eyes. Turned to face the wall of dirt. Stretched her arms and stuck out her hands.

His fingers were about six inches above.

Her feet descended into water, cold water. It chilled her feet and then her ankles. Her heels sank into soggy mud. One shoe fell off. Mud oozed between her toes. It felt icky.

"Sorry," Thad said. "I didn't think the soil near the edge was so weak." He stuck his hand farther down. She strained but still couldn't reach it. Mud pulled at her feet. More dirt fell and rolled down her back. Would the hole collapse and swallow her? She panted, taking short breaths. Her stomach churned. Was she going to be buried alive?

She wasn't ready to die. She hadn't even made a mark as an attorney. She hadn't traveled, seen other countries. There were things she wanted to do—like ziplining and parasailing.

"Hey, anybody home?" Joe called. "Mr. Thayer, why are you lying on the ground? Are you hurt?"

"No. Don't come any closer. The ground's unstable. Kayla fell into the sinkhole. I'm trying to pull her out. Can you call 911?"

Kayla let out her breath. Joe was here. Thank goodness. Maybe they could pull her out before the hole collapsed.

"No time for that," Joe said. "Do you have any rope?"

Down in the hole, Kayla stared up.

"Hang on, Kayla, I've got some rope in the garage," Thad said. His face and arms disappeared as he pulled away. His clothes rustled as he inched over dry grass away from the hole.

Hopefully, the two of them could get her out. She brushed hair from her face and glanced at her wrinkled suit. Rubbing her fingers over her face, she hoped she'd brushed off any dirt.

"How did you manage to fall down there?" Joe asked.

"I stood too close, and the soil fell away."

"Here's some rope." Thad held it out. "What do you think's the best way to do this?"

"You lie down behind me," Joe said. "I'll lie prone next to the hole and extend the rope. Hang on to my feet. I'll tie knots so she'll have something to hold on to."

"Good thought," Thad said.

Joe's face appeared above the hole. He dangled the rope with knots. She grabbed hold and held on tight.

"Ready to get out of there?" Joe asked.

"Am I ever." She moved her foot around, trying to find her shoe, then gave up. It was a lost cause. The rope pulled at her hands and then her arms. Clods of dirt fell away as Joe pulled her up. She turned her face away to avoid the dirt.

Finally, her head was above the hole. Grass never smelled so sweet. Joe grabbed her hands. She felt the strength of his muscles as he pulled. His hands grasping hers were sure and steady.

More clods fell as she was pulled over the dry grass and then onto greener, softer blades. As her feet cleared the hole, she wanted to get up on her knees but didn't trust the ground beneath.

The chill from her wet feet moved up, and she shivered. What she wouldn't give for a nice hot shower right now. Joe rose up on his knees but kept hold of her hands. "I think it's safe to stand up here."

Kayla stood, picked up her camera, and brushed off her clothes. "Thanks, guys, for saving my life." Oh, my gosh. How awful she must look. One shoe was missing. Her pantyhose were dirty and streaked with runs. Her suit would never be the same again.

"It's so embarrassing to have you see me like this. Never again will I wish a hole would swallow me up." She glanced back at the sinkhole. "I've had enough of that for real. Joe, I'm so glad you came out. Why did you change your mind?"

"I didn't believe the hole was enlarging that fast, so I wanted to see for myself." He shook his head. "But never mind that. I thought I was going to lose you." He looked her over and touched her arm. "Are you all right?"

That felt comforting, and she was heartened by his concern. He must really care about her. "I'm okay." She tried to smooth her hair, but it was all knotted and dirty.

"I'm sorry," Thad said. "I shouldn't have asked you to come."

"Well, I'm okay, thanks to you two." She shivered.

"Kayla, you must be cold," Joe said. "I've got a windbreaker in my car. Let me get it for you."

"No thanks. I need to go home and change." She picked up her purse from the chair in the patio. "Thad, I'll call you after I speak with the court clerk."

"Okay. I'll put this rope away. Hopefully, I won't need it for something like that again." He went inside his back door.

Joe touched her shoulder. "Sure you didn't break a bone or sprain an ankle? Maybe you should see a doctor."

She wriggled her bare foot. It seemed okay. She took

off her lone shoe. "I'll be fine as soon as I can take a hot shower." Joe walked her to her car. She unlocked it, got in, and rolled down the window.

Joe stood beside her, his expression solemn. "I was really worried about you, imagining all that dirt falling on you. Or water sucking you down. If you died, I would be always thinking what else I might have done to save you. That would dwell in my thoughts forever."

He grasped her hand and squeezed it. "I'm so glad you're all right. There are lots of places I'd like to take you and things we could do after those two cases are settled."

Kayla couldn't help smiling. "I'm looking forward to that." She waved goodbye and drove to her apartment. She'd felt the strength in Joe's arms as he pulled. And it was nice to hear how much he cared. What he'd said surprised her, but she was sure he meant every word.

Inside her living room, she called Beth, explained what happened, and said she'd be in after a while. Later, in her shower, hot water cascaded down her shoulders and back, warming her at last. She rubbed soap all over, hoping she got all the dirt and germs off. Just remembering her feet stuck in the cold water with mud oozing over her feet sent a chill down her spine. She washed her hair, stayed under the hot water until she was toasty warm, and then blow-dried her hair.

Once at her office, feeling better after her shower and a change of clothes, she called the court clerk. "Has the judge set a court date yet for *Thayer vs. Black*?" She stated the case number.

"Sorry, but I don't see it on the docket."

"The sinkhole is getting bigger every day and threatening my client's house. Would you please explain that to the person who schedules the cases? I need this case heard as soon as possible."

"There are cases that already have a court date set. There is nothing available for at least a month. I'll notify your office when the date is set. My other line is ringing, so I have to answer it."

"Would you please let me know when a date's available?" Kayla gave the clerk her phone number and said goodbye.

She called Thad and told him the bad news.

Thad sighed. "I guess I'll just have to get a contractor started on filling the sinkhole and trust you to get a good deal for me."

"Since we can't get a trial date soon, I may up your settlement demand and do my best to win the case," she said and hung up, determined to move this case along as quickly as possible.

The next morning, Kayla called Beth into her office. "Do you have the interrogatories and request for production responses on the sinkhole case typed up for Joe Morales?"

Beth nodded. "Do you want me to send them by e-mail or fax them?"

"Neither. I'll take them over myself. Please get me an appointment."

"Yes." Beth headed back to her desk. A few minutes later, she returned. "He'll see you at one o'clock."

After lunch, Kayla entered Joe's office and walked across the caramel-colored carpet. Anne led her to his office. Kayla held out the papers. "Here's some discovery documents for *Thayer vs. Black*."

Joe rose. "You didn't need to bring those over in person."

Kayla laid them on his desk. "I wanted to thank you again for saving my life. Down in that hole, I was scared I might get sucked under or buried with all that dirt."

He smiled. "I was glad to do it. Sure didn't want to face some other attorney from your firm." He winked at her.

Kayla swallowed. Now, after all he'd done and how concerned he acted, she'd have to put on her war hat and be his adversary again. "Did your client admit to stealing my research notes?"

Leaning over the desk in his chair, Joe lowered his chin. "If he had, I couldn't tell you, but I asked, and he denied it."

Kayla frowned. "I already went online and redid the research, but I would like the material back. I suppose whoever stole them tossed them in a dumpster. If I find out it was your client, I could have him charged with contempt of court. I hope you explained the consequences of destroying evidence."

"I did, and he still insisted he was innocent."

"Whoever it was stole a pillowcase that was part of a new matching pair."

"I'll buy you a new set. That's the least I can do to make up for your trouble."

"No. You don't have to do that." She pointed to the discovery documents she'd set on his desk. "I'd appreciate your replies before the required thirty days. My client needs to have his property fixed as soon as possible and can't wait forever for reimbursement."

Joe gave her a stern look. "I have other cases I need to take care of besides yours, but you'll get them in thirty days."

She glared at him, wanting to show him she meant

business. "In that case, I'll get back to my office. I'm also drafting a divorce decree for the Witherspoons, which I'll send you shortly."

Joe frowned. "My client won't agree to any more demands, so don't try to add one. Your demand for college funds is way too high. He's not paying for her to obtain an enriched education."

Kayla rose and pointed a finger at him. "Have you forgotten his daughter? His wife, soon-to-be ex-wife, needs money for college, and I intend to see that he pays for it all."

"Like hell he will. She's getting to stay in the house. He insists his wife is able-bodied and should get a job."

"How's she supposed to get a decent job without any education or training?"

"Plenty of jobs don't require more than a high school education. Why should she sit on her butt and study, when she could work at some store?"

"That would require long hours away from their child and tire her out so she'd have a hard time giving their daughter the attention she needs."

"So? She wanted this divorce, and he didn't. I guess she'll have to live with the consequences."

When Joe turned obnoxious, he didn't pull any punches. She shot him a stern look, turned, and marched out of his office, down the hall, and through the reception area without looking backward.

As she got in her car, she gritted her teeth. Why had she ever thought he was attractive and charming? He was just another lawyer, determined to get his way. Well, she could be determined, too. She'd get justice for both her clients he opposed.

The next day, Joe called her. "I questioned the nurse

at the hospital about the man who brought the threatening note, and she described Thad Thayer right down to his auburn hair and mustache."

She'd suspected Thad had sent the note, but due to attorney-client privilege, she shouldn't say anything.

"I should report that to the police," he said.

"And what good would that do unless you have fingerprints? Your developer is still responsible for fixing the sinkhole. He never provided the core sample I requested. I'm betting he doesn't have one."

"But he took core samples for many of the lots. I'll ask him to check again before the trial."

"I won't believe he took one there until I see the report."

That evening, Kayla had just finished her shower and put on a robe when the doorbell rang.

She went to the door and asked, "Who is it?"

"Clay. Open up. Want to talk with you."

Oh, no. She groaned. She had been firm with him, but he was being a jerk. "It's late, and we have nothing to talk about."

"Uh—open the door. You got something to drink? Beer, Coke?"

She opened the door a crack but kept the chain on. He reeked of alcohol. His shirt was rumpled, and his eyes were bleary. "I think you've had plenty to drink."

"Want to talk…'bout you an' me. 'Bout getting back together."

"No, Clay. It's not going to happen. I'm seeing someone else." Not exactly true, but she wanted to get rid of him.

"Who? That lawyer fella you're hanging around?"

"That's none of your business."

"Why did you break up with me? I miss your kisses. Best I've had since I saw you last."

"Not only did you cheat on me, I didn't have time to see you anymore. I had to concentrate on finishing law school. You wouldn't believe how hard I had to study to even make a B in some of those classes." Why had she ever put up with him as long as she had?

"Always knew you was smart. Aw, Kayla, you look sexy in that robe." He reached under the chain toward her robe.

Naked underneath, she backed away.

"Always liked feeling you up, and now, I wanta fuck you like you never been fucked. And you're gonna love it."

"You'd better leave me alone from now on. If you don't, I'll file a restraining order against you. I can call the police if you come near me again."

"What? You'd really do that?"

"Damn right I will if you come near me again. It's time you left." Now, she worried he'd try to drive. "You'd better call an Uber to take you home." She shut the door and locked it. After a moment, relieved at the sounds of his shuffling feet, she hoped that was the last she'd see of him.

****

Joe sat at an oak table facing the judge, waiting for the cursed sinkhole case to begin. Last week, he'd spent an hour dictating answers to Kayla's interrogatory questions and had Anne make copies of documents Kayla had requested and had them hand delivered. Man, she was thorough. Too bad, he didn't have any evidence he could send to the court at the last minute to send her scurrying to refute.

Behind the male judge in black robes, a chrome-framed clock ticked loud enough to hear above the whispers of the spectators on wooden benches. Sunlight shone through the windows, illuminating dust motes floating in the air. Joe tapped his fingers on the table. His client still hadn't provided a core sample for Thayer's property, but Joe had core sample reports from several properties in the development. He hoped that would be enough to win a jury made up of small business owners, two apartment dwellers, one house owner, a teacher, and a librarian.

Kayla appeared in court, polished and confident in a navy suit and heels. Her white blouse hinted at her luscious curves, which he shouldn't be thinking about now. She set a bulging briefcase on the table in front of her. Her client wore a sports jacket and well-pressed pants, but Joe couldn't keep his eyes off Kayla. Once this trial was over, he could ask her out. He'd never asked what kind of movies she liked or if she'd like to go dancing. He could hardly wait for this trial to be finished.

After the opening arguments, Joe called a geologist as a witness. The man reported none of the core samples presented showed the type of soil likely to develop sinkholes. Joe leaned back. He hoped that was enough.

Kayla presented enlarged pictures and data showing the sinkhole was gradually getting larger. Then she mentioned that Richard Black had never done a core sample on Thad Thayer's property before building the house and selling it to him.

She made a thorough, persuasive presentation, and the jurors seemed to be paying attention. Several appeared sympathetic. Damn it. Then she talked about the damage this sinkhole could do to her client's house and described how she'd fallen into it. Several jurors nodded. After she'd described an extreme possibility, one shook his head.

Then the case went to the jury, and everyone walked out of the courtroom. Joe sat with his client on a bench in the hall, and she sat with hers on a separate bench opposite them.

Joe beckoned to Kayla. "Would you please step back inside the courtroom with me? I want to ask you something."

She rose and followed him into the courtroom. Over the judge's desk, a big clock ticked loudly.

Joe faced her. "Well, it will soon be over." He smiled. "Since we won't be on opposing sides anymore, except for the final divorce hearing, why don't we bet a nice dinner on the outcome, with the loser paying for it?"

Kayla nodded. "Sure. I'd love for you to feed me a steak dinner."

Joe grinned. "I've heard of brides and grooms feeding each other cake, but feeding you steak would be different. You'd probably grasp my hand to pull the fork to your mouth faster."

Kayla laughed. "Are you calling me greedy?"

Joe shook his head. "Of course not. I wouldn't dare. You might bite the hand that feeds you."

"Hey, if you're paying for dinner, I'd be happy to feed myself as long as it's a big steak. I don't want one of those dainty seven-ounce ones."

"I'm willing to bet you'll be buying, but I'll let you choose the restaurant if I lose, which, of course, I won't." He winked at her.

"I like Outback Steakhouse. I love their rib eye

steaks."

"But I'm going to win, so we'll eat at Olive Garden. I love Italian."

They walked out of the courtroom to sit with their respective clients. For an hour, he kept assuring his client they had a strong case and should win.

Finally, the bailiff stepped out into the hall and announced the jury had returned. Joe patted Richard Black's shoulder. "I believe we'll win." Joe sat beside his client at the table, slid his hand under the table, and crossed his fingers. He'd presented a good case for a natural anomaly, but that might not fly. Studying the jurors' solemn faces told him nothing.

Chapter Eight

The foreman of the jury rose. "We find the defendant guilty of not providing proper evaluation of the property before building a house and selling it to Thad Thayer. We also find his request for five hundred thousand dollars in damages an equitable settlement for Mr. Thayer."

Joe drew in a deep breath. He couldn't believe it. He'd lost. Big-time. And his client had to pay.

He swallowed, the ache in his throat making it hard to speak. "I'm sorry, Richard. I thought we had this case sewed up." He'd send his client a bill and hope he paid all of it. He followed Richard Black out of the courtroom and led him to a bench. "I'll return in a moment."

He hadn't won the case, but at least he'd get to take Kayla out to dinner. He went back into the courtroom to talk quietly with her. "I'll call you later about dinner."

She had a wide smile on her face. "I still want to go to Outback, and I'll have the twelve-ounce rib eye steak. You can pick the date."

Richard appeared in the courtroom doorway. "You lost the case, and you're taking your opponent out to dinner? What's the deal? I thought attorneys on a case were not supposed to fraternize."

Joe drew in a deep breath, trying to ignore the ache in his chest. "I'm sorry. I was so sure we'd win, I bet her the loser of the case would buy the other one dinner."

Richard scowled. "A fine attorney you are. I'll pay your damn exorbitant bill, but from now on, someone else will handle my legal business." He marched down the hall and left the building.

Damn. It was bad enough to lose the case, but he had to lose the client, too. Trying to ignore his churning stomach, Joe trudged out of the building and walked to his car. The parking garage had been full, and he'd had to park on the street. Looking down, he walked to his car.

"Damn." This was the first case he'd lost since he'd moved from San Antonio to Dallas. He hated the debilitation descending on him. Even more, he hated feeling inadequate. He'd worked hours on this case, studied over fifteen core sample reports from the subdivision, and thought that was enough to prove his client had made a reasonable effort to check out the properties. *He had more experience than Kayla. Still, he'd lost. Maybe I'm not as good as I thought I was. Maybe I need to work harder and take advice from my partner, Matt. He's been a lawyer much longer than I.*

He wanted to go home. Didn't want to face whatever work he had at the office. It would still be there when he returned. Hopefully, he'd be in a better mood to tackle it.

He called his legal assistant. "Anne, I won't be coming back to the office today. Tell anyone who calls I'll get back with them tomorrow." He hoped after a few beers and going for a run he'd be over this funk.

He still had to take smart, sexy Kayla to dinner. How could he still be attracted to someone who'd beaten him so badly in court?

The next morning, while Joe was filing a petition at

the courthouse, he ran into Kayla.

"When are you going to take me for that steak dinner we bet on?"

"I'm tied up until the weekend," he said, "but I'll call you later, and we can set a date."

"I'm looking forward to it. I'll enjoy watching you eat humble pie."

He groaned. Apparently, she couldn't resist needling him. "You don't have to rub it in. Hey, I've got to get back to the office, but I'll check my calendar." He pulled out his phone and tapped on it. But the phone rang, and he answered. "Hello, Ellen. I'm not interested in going anywhere with you, so please don't call me again."

"Wait. Don't hang up," Ellen said. "I'm in terrible trouble."

He faced Kayla. "Hang on. I'll finish with her in a moment." He spoke into the phone. "Can't you call another lawyer?"

"You know Robert Mundy?"

"What about him?"

"He's threatening to blackmail me."

"What does he want?"

"Fifty thousand dollars."

Joe leaned against a wall. "Fifty thousand?"

Kayla gasped.

Joe gulped. "What does he have on you?"

"N-naked pictures of me. He's threatening to send them to a tabloid and put them on the Internet. I can't have that. It will ruin my reputation and make it impossible to get a job."

"I see why you're worried. You could file a restraining order against him."

"That won't deter him. Please. I need you to stop him, or I won't be able to—" She broke into sobs.

"Ellen, I'm at the courthouse, and I need to get back to my office. I've a lot to keep me busy, and I'd rather not get involved. Why don't you call my partner, Matt Larson? He's good at facing down assholes like Mundy."

"Okay. I'll call him."

Joe disconnected.

Kayla looked at him. "I thought you were through with her."

Joe explained. "My ex, and I do mean ex-girlfriend, is being threatened by a former crooked cop. He's one I arranged to get busted."

"I see. Could this be a ploy to get you to hook up with her again?"

He frowned. Why would Kayla immediately think that? Of course, it might be, but Ellen sounded frantic, like she really needed help. "I couldn't see letting ex-officer Mundy threaten her. That's why I recommended she see Matt. I'll get back to you later about the steak dinner."

His life had seemed so much better after meeting Kayla. She really seemed to like him, and she was everything he could want in a girlfriend. Too bad she was jealous of Ellen when she didn't need to be. If Kayla wasn't interested in him, his life wouldn't seem as bright.

When he returned to his office, Ellen was waiting in the outer office. She wore a low-necked sweater that showed off her boobs to good advantage. A heavy wave of her perfume assailed him as he said hello and walked past her. Anne had mentioned earlier that Ellen had made an appointment with Matt. Joe drew in a deep breath. He really didn't want to see her again, but she needed help, and he didn't want Robert Mundy to be enriched. Joe hoped Matt would get Mundy to leave her alone.

A few minutes later, Ellen paused in front of his office. She stepped in, smiled coyly, and showed him a snapshot of her lying naked on a bed. "This is a copy of the picture that slimeball is threatening to post on the Internet."

Neither a glance at the photo nor her smiling face affected him like it might have when they were dating. Her manipulating ways had grated on him, and that's why he'd broken up with her.

She smiled at him. "Would you like to meet me for drinks after work?"

Joe shook his head. "Sorry, I've got other plans."

He opened a file on his desk, hoping she'd take the hint.

Finally, she sashayed to the hallway, her hips swinging as she headed toward Matt's office.

He sighed and hoped that was the end of his dealings with Ellen. He asked Anne to get Kayla on the phone. Things often worked out better face-to-face, but he didn't have time to go to her office. Besides, that could put him at a disadvantage. Maybe he could get her and Mrs. Witherspoon to agree to final divorce decree stipulations. Anne buzzed him. "Kayla Walker is on the line." He picked up his desk phone.

****

"Hello, Joe. My client is holding out for four years' support while she goes to college."

"But it shouldn't take that long. You said she quit college to get married, but surely she has some credits."

"It's been five years. They may not accept them at

Texas Women's University. She wants to get a degree as well as an RN."

"Well, I'll discuss it with her husband and let you know, but I don't think he'll budge on that. He says it will limit what he can do with his business."

"Too bad if it cramps his style. He should have thought of that before cheating on his wife. By the way, I picked up a new client yesterday. His name's Pierce. He's a scruffy guy with a misdemeanor charge. Since he moved here from San Antonio, I wonder if you might have heard of him?"

"I never met the guy, but one of the men that kidnapped Matt's wife before they married was named Pierce. He was arrested and got out on bail, but then skipped town. There's a warrant for his arrest. They charged him with aggravated kidnapping, a first-degree felony, which will cost him twenty years."

"Pierce is a common name, but it's probably not the same guy. Even if this man has been accused of a felony, he needs an attorney."

"If it's the same guy, I'm sure he had one in San Antonio. Probably skipped out on paying him. You'd better check his record to see if he's a client you really want to take on. He might be dangerous. What if you don't win the case, and he comes after you?"

"That's ridiculous. He doesn't seem the type at all. He even was on time for his first appointment for a third-degree misdemeanor. This man acts so grateful to have an attorney represent him. He brought me coffee and a doughnut the first time he came in. I don't think he'd harm me, even if I lose the case for him. I told him I'd check into his record and see him next Thursday."

"Well, I defended a very mild-mannered man for

killing a cop. I thought he was innocent. Everyone who knew him said he wasn't likely to kill anyone, but he was out on parole and didn't want to go back to jail when a cop stopped him. However, the prosecutor produced a bodycam worn by the dead officer showing the shooting. You shouldn't represent this man, especially if it turns out he's the one that helped kidnap Matt's wife."

Kayla frowned. "Don't tell me what to do or not do. I plan to represent him. He deserves a fair trial."

"Hey, it's your client and your case. I just wanted to warn you about possible dangers."

"Nothing's going to happen. I'll only see him in my office. Since he's not coming in until the end of next week, I'll have time to check his record."

"I just wanted you to be aware, but be careful. How about going out tonight for that steak dinner I promised you?"

"It's Columbus Day. The law firm I work for is having a holiday picnic at a lake, and I'd better be there."

"Well, then, how about going with me to a movie afterward?"

"Yes, I'd like to go after the picnic."

Later that day, Laura, her friend and attorney in the adjoining office, stepped into Kayla's office. "You ready to leave for the company picnic?"

Kayla put the paper she was reading back on the pile on her desk. "I will in a moment. Don't know why we don't just have the day off like other businesses."

"I heard the head partner thought it would make for more comradery among us, for whatever that's worth. Most of the attorneys have already left for Joe Pool Lake. Hope you brought your swimsuit."

Kayla shook her head. "I don't want to swim. I just

brought shorts and a T-shirt." She picked up a piece of paper. "I need to finish this first. Go on ahead. I know the way."

Laura laughed. "You're a glutton for punishment. Our paralegal has already left and so have most of the attorneys. The cleaning crew should be here any minute now."

"See you there," Kayla said as Laura walked out.

After jotting down notes for tasks to finish tomorrow, Kayla gathered her shorts and T-shirt and headed for the ladies' room. After changing, she walked back to her office. Except for the low whine of a vacuum somewhere down the hall, things seemed quiet. She set her neatly folded suit and blouse on her desk. As she pulled her purse from a desk drawer, the jangle of the phone startled her. She debated letting the answering service take it, but maybe one of her clients had an urgent question. She set down her purse and grabbed the phone.

It was Pierce. "There's a warrant out for my arrest. I don't know what to do. Can I come talk to you now?"

"I was about to leave for a company picnic, and you're not scheduled until Thursday. Can you come in tomorrow? I can make time for you then."

"I'm afraid to go home. My roommate said a cop came there with a warrant looking for me. He might come back."

"You really should go give yourself in."

"Please let me come see you. I can be there real soon."

"Okay, but you can't stay long. I have somewhere to go."

"Sure, I understand."

She sat down at her desk, and true to his word, the

short, stocky man in need of a shave walked in. He must have been outside in his car when he called. "You have to help me. Can you get them to ditch the warrant for my arrest?"

She walked around her desk to stand before him. "What are you charged with?"

He looked down. "Breaking and entering, but the back door was unlocked. It wasn't like I broke in. Some damn neighbor must have seen me and reported it."

"But you went in without an invitation. That's still breaking and entering. Did you take anything?"

"They didn't have much. All I found was a fifty and a few one-dollar bills lying on the table in the front hallway."

"Hey, was that one of the two fifty-dollar bills you gave me as a retainer?"

He nodded. Great. Now the bill in her wallet was evidence. "You should turn yourself in."

He stepped closer, his bulk shadowing her. "Will you come to the police station with me now and talk them into releasing me until trial, and later help get me probation?"

She didn't like the way he was insisting she do something immediately. She looked straight at him, trying to ignore his size and muscled arms. "What makes you think I could do that? Even if you confess, return the money, and say you're sorry, I can't guarantee they'll agree to that."

She caught her breath. He scared her to death, but she had to talk some sense into him. "So, are you going to turn yourself in?"

He frowned and stepped closer. "Hell, no."

Kayla bit her lip, then realized that would look

weak. "You're in my space. Please step back."

"I might as well leave town with whatever money I can scrounge up, including the hundred I paid you." He grabbed her purse from her desk.

She reached for it and tugged the strap.

It fell open, letting her wallet and keys drop to the floor.

Scared he'd leave her without transportation, she grabbed the keys and reached for her wallet.

"Give me your wallet and your keys."

She clutched them to her chest. "No."

He grabbed her wrist and bent her arm behind her.

The sharp pain made it hard to concentrate. Damn. Why hadn't she listened to Joe and checked this guy out sooner? "Hey, let go of my arm. Ow. That hurts. I won't represent you if you don't let go." Of course, she wouldn't now. She'd file an assault charge.

He lessened the pull on her arm but didn't let go. Her stomach clenched. He put his face close to hers. His drunken breath made her gag.

He glared at her. Dark eyes and an evil grin taunted her. "Everyone but you is gone now."

Holding her wallet against her chest, she gripped her keys so tightly her knuckles turned white. She hoped the cleaning crew was nearby. "Help! I'm being attacked. Help!"

She kicked his shins.

"Stop that, bitch."

"You're nothing but a common criminal." He must be the guy who kidnapped Joe's partner's wife and skipped bail.

"Give me your car keys. I need to get out of town. The cops probably have my car license plate number."

Her throat tightened. She kicked him again. Tried to wrestle her arm free. He twisted harder. Felt like he was wrenching it out of her socket. "Help!" she screamed.

No one came.

She clenched her teeth and inched toward her purse. Her father had programed 911 into her phone. She needed to grab it from the outside pocket. Of course, that side faced the carpet. Drat the bad luck.

She stuck her foot out. Tried to tip the purse over.

"Oh, no, you don't." Pierce shoved it out of reach. He twisted her around. Reached for her keys.

With no pockets, she dropped them down her neckline. Faced his scowl with one of her own.

He let go of one arm. She struggled. He held the other tightly. Reached in his pocket. Pulled out zip ties and shoved her to her knees. Tied her wrists together. Was he going to kill her?

"Help!" she screamed again.

A vacuum cleaner sounded somewhere in the building, but nobody came. Her heart thumped against her ribs. If only whoever was running it would come, she'd get help.

"Gimme those keys." Pierce stuck a hand down her neckline. She tried to move back, but the dirty bum shoved his hand right down her neckline. How disgusting and humiliating. She tensed and shivered.

Where the hell was the cleaning crew?

Chapter Nine

Pierce's rough fingers fumbled deeper between her bra and her flesh. She shivered. The keys slipped down farther. Got caught in the waistband of her shorts.

She bit his arm. And screamed. Running footsteps sounded.

"Screw you, bitch," he said. He grabbed her purse and wallet and ran out the door.

A lean, gray-haired janitor hurried in. "Do you need help, miss?"

"A man just robbed me. Call security for me." She recited the numbers. "There's a phone on my desk." Rotating her shoulders, she tried to stand.

The janitor grabbed the phone and punched in numbers. He reported what she'd said and put the phone down. "Are you all right, miss?"

She sighed. "I guess I am now, except for these zip ties. I've heard you can break them by swinging your arms up and down, but he tied my arms behind my back so I can't do that."

"I'm sorry he did that. Wait a minute." He pulled out a pocketknife. "Now, turn around."

She felt a sharp pull, and then she was free. "Thanks." She pulled her keys from the waistband of her shorts and stretched out her arms. They ached, but it felt good to move them freely.

"If you're all right, ma'am, I'll just stay until

someone from security comes, and then I have to finish my work."

"That will be fine. Thanks again for coming to help."

A few minutes later, the security guard walked in. "What happened?"

Kayla told him as the janitor left.

"Lock the door behind me and call the police. I'll see if he's still around." He hurried out.

Still shaken, Kayla collapsed onto her desk chair. After calling the police, she gave them his name, a description, and his address, then hung up.

Her work clothes lay where she'd left them on her desk. She wasn't in the mood for a company picnic. Besides, she had to call all her credit card companies to cancel her cards before driving home.

She had just finished calling the last one when Joe walked in.

"Hi, how was the company picnic?"

"I didn't go." She explained what happened.

"I'm so sorry you had to go through that. Are you all right?"

"Yeah, I guess so, but all I want to do tonight is to drive home and go to bed. Can I have a rain check on the movie?"

"I can follow you to be sure you're all right. Would you like me to have some Chinese food delivered?"

"Sure. I like Chinese, but don't get anything too spicy."

"How about sweet and sour chicken?"

"That would be great."

He took her hand, walked with her to her car, and waited until she was behind the wheel. "I'll follow you."

Luckily, when she reached the parking garage, there were two vacant spaces near each other. After they parked, Joe walked with her into the building. "The food should arrive soon after we get there."

And it did. Joe met the delivery guy at the door, paid him, and took the package into her kitchen. He transferred the food to plates and set them on her table with knives and forks from her drawers.

How nice it was to have him take care of her like this.

As they ate, Joe reached over and touched her arm, sending a sizzle up it. "Are you sure you're all right? Would you like me to take you to a clinic or the ER to have a doctor check you over?"

Kayla shook her head. "My arms ache a bit, but I'm sure I didn't break any bones."

"That's good. I remember falling out of a tree when my brother dared me to step out further on a skinny branch." He grinned. "I couldn't resist a dare."

"Bet you were sorry afterward."

"I remember seeing my mother run from the house in a panic. As I told her I was okay, I realized how much she loved me. That made up for my aches and pains. She seemed really anxious as she'd dragged me to the car and drove me to the doctor."

"So, did you break anything?"

He shook his head. "My aches and pains went away in a few days, and I hope yours will, too."

After they ate, he helped her wash the dishes. Then he took her in his arms, held her gently, and kissed her. What started out as a tender kiss grew deeper. She threw her arms around his neck and responded eagerly. And the sparks, no, make that flames, still burned bright.

His mouth roved over hers until he finally broke away. "I guess I'd better let you get some rest. Sleep tight, and I'll call you tomorrow. Good night."

As he walked to the elevator, she realized he hadn't once said, "I told you so."

****

The next morning at work, after explaining what happened to Laura and the managing partner, Kayla sipped her coffee, still thinking about last night. Pierce had her wallet, her driver's license, and worst of all, her address. Would he try to break into her condo? Luckily, a security force manned the front desk in the building lobby, and the back entrance required a code to enter.

Beth buzzed her. "Joe Morales is on the phone for you."

Kayla picked it up.

"How are you? I hope you don't have any lingering aches and pains."

"I'm okay now."

"I'll be driving to Austin this morning, but I'll call you when I'm back in Dallas and take you for that steak dinner."

"Since I'm driving to Austin today to take part in the march—"

"What march?"

"We're marching to raise the legislature's awareness of the importance of increasing the area of the state park near Dallas. We want the bill to pass."

"There's a lot of opposition to that. My client, or rather ex-client, Richard Black, and all the area developers and builders are adamantly against it."

"I can imagine they would be. Building houses to get more dollars is more important to them than preserving the land for nature's creatures."

"There is plenty of land in the park as it is. Those developers and builders have a powerful alliance and a strong will to prevent that bill from passing. One legislator has already received threats. I'm not sure it's safe for you to take part in a march in Austin."

"It's not really a protest march. It's more like a parade of people who support keeping the ecological balance as intact as possible."

"Well, protest marches have gotten ugly in Portland, in Seattle, in Kenosha, Wisconsin."

"But those were not in Texas."

"Remember the one in Dallas when a man shot five police officers. I wish you'd reconsider."

"Well, I feel strongly about this, so I'm taking part. But I strongly encourage you to vote for it. As I was going to say before you interrupted me, after the protest march would be a good time for you to pay off your bet to take me to dinner. I understand there's an Outback restaurant in Austin."

"Fine. I'll take you there tonight after your march." He sounded grouchy but protective as well. It was comforting to have someone concerned about her safety, but she didn't think there'd be any problems during the march.

Kayla gave Beth instructions, then put the finishing touches on her poster for the Ecological Preservation Association. Noting the initials were EPA, she smiled.

During the three-hour drive to Austin, Kayla thought about Joe's assumptions about the march. Surely, he was being overly pessimistic. Would he be in a good mood and friendly when he took her out to dinner? Since the sinkhole case was over, maybe they could finally date. When he smiled at her, it made her feel really alive, and the whole world seemed rosier. He was by far the most interesting man she'd come in contact with. Vivid memories of their closest contact made her want to be that close again.

She left her car a few blocks away where there were no parking meters. Finally, she reached the area where people were assembling for the march. Other participants waved colorful posters. Some wore hats with homemade figurines resembling birds, bats, muskrats, javelinas, or armadillos. One person even had a likeness of a ground squirrel with many stripes, which resembled a chipmunk. Many carried signs saying, "Stop the extinction of native animals."

Holding her poster, she lined up behind those at the front, and a band started playing "What a Wonderful World" to enthuse everyone. She started walking with the crowd. Marching up Congress Avenue toward the pink granite capitol building, with its dome resembling the national capitol in Washington, D.C., should be easy and peaceful.

Something smashed a mailbox on the sidewalk beside her. It spewed flames. Her sleeve caught on fire. Burned her arm and hurt like hell.

People around her shouted. Everyone scattered in all directions. A man bumped into her. She fell. The poster flew from her hands. The harsh concrete scraped her palms.

Her arm burned. Legs ran by. She thrust her arms away from her head. Scrambled between runners to the side of the road. Rolled her arm in the grass. That put out the fire. The pain was horrendous. She felt dizzy, like being twirled in a whirlpool.

She sat cross-legged on the grass. Loud sirens heralded the approach of the fire department and an ambulance. People hurried to get out of the way. After the vehicle stopped, a paramedic rushed over. He asked questions. Her pain pounded. It was hard to answer. She held out her arm. "I got burned. By a Molotov cocktail, I think."

"We can take you to the emergency room. That okay with you, miss?"

She bit her lip to keep from crying out. "Yes," she finally got out and tried to rise.

The paramedic held her uninjured arm and helped her stand. Another paramedic wheeled a gurney over to her.

She shook her head. "I think I can walk."

As they lifted her up into the ambulance, camera flashes went off. This wasn't how she wanted to be on the news.

Inside, they treated her burn with something that stung, and urged her to lie still while the paramedic put antiseptic on her bruised knee, checked her blood pressure, and inserted an IV. She shivered. "I'm cold." The paramedic put a blanket over her, and she felt the vehicle start to move.

The ambulance sped off without a siren. She must not be in danger of dying. Seemed to take a long time to get to the hospital. What if that injury made it hard to use her right arm? Thank goodness she was an attorney and not a paralegal. Her legal assistant would do the typing for her, but even so, she didn't want to lose any mobility in her arm.

Later, she lay in a hospital bed, feeling alone in a room with cream-colored walls. The picture of a flower-filled garden only made her wish she was home at her Dallas apartment with flower pots on the balcony. At least there, she'd have friends and family to visit her. The reddened and blistered flesh on her right arm looked awful. Her whole arm hurt, but at least her fingers worked.

Antiseptic smells filled the air as a nurse in pink scrubs treated her arm.

"Will I have a terrible scar?"

"You have a second-degree burn, which may affect the underneath layer of skin. You'll blister and hurt, but it's less likely to scar. You'll need to apply Silvedene cream and change the bandages often."

Kayla shivered. "It's cold in here."

"I'll be right back with another heated blanket."

When the nurse returned, she said, "Leave your burned arm exposed to the air." She laid the warm blanket over the rest of Kayla's body. Now she felt warm all over.

"The doctor said you can leave later tonight," the nurse said, "but do not drive back to Dallas. It's best if you have someone you can stay with." The nurse walked out.

Kayla thought of calling her dad, who rented an apartment in Austin while the legislature was in session, but decided not to. Turning her attention away from her arm, she focused on a picture of a placid lake with a patch of black-eyed Susans on the shore. Feeling drowsy, she drifted off to sleep.

She awoke to see Joe sitting in a chair across from her bed. She blinked. What a wonderful surprise. "When did you get here? How did you know I got hurt?"

"I caught a news update on my phone and saw you

being lifted into an ambulance. I'm sorry you got injured." He glanced at her burned arm. "That looks nasty."

He ran his fingers down her other arm. It felt comforting. "How are you feeling?"

"My arm still hurts, but they gave me something for the pain." The skin on her arm appeared blotchy, redder in some spots than others. Her arm was swollen and had blisters. "I hope I don't have a big scar."

"It looks bad now, but a scar won't matter to me. The rest of you is beautiful."

That warmed her heart. This guy sure knew how to make her feel better. And he hadn't even brought up his warning not to be in the march or said, "I told you so."

Joe glanced over at her. "You can't imagine how shocked I was when I recognized you being helped on a gurney. I could see your eyes were open, but I couldn't tell how badly you were injured."

His expression turned solemn. "I had horrible thoughts of you dying on the way to the hospital. I was worried I wouldn't be able to spend any more time with you. I really worried you weren't going to make it—"

Kayla opened her eyes wider. His words warmed her heart. She hadn't realized he cared about her that much. Maybe he wasn't averse to a relationship with a forceful, professional woman like her.

And he'd made a special trip to see her. That made her smile. "I hope my arm soon gets back to normal, but the nurse says I may not know until it heals."

He patted her hand. "And if you recover the full use of your arm, that's all anyone should care about. I brought you something." He held out a big box of Whitman's Sampler chocolates.

Opening it, she smiled. "Thank you so much." She took one and held out the box. "Help yourself." This guy was worth holding on to and keeping. Hopefully, she wouldn't have any more cases where he was the opposing attorney.

"I'll bring you a book. What would you like?"

"A romantic suspense by Brenda Novak or a thriller by Lisa Jackson or even a David Baldacci book would be great."

He wrote something on a notepad. "I want to tell you about the crazy speech some pompous ass from the other party made during today's session." Joe kept her laughing with the story and other tales from behind the scenes of the legislature. Thankfully that distracted her from the pain.

After about an hour, a nurse came in to take her blood pressure and her temperature. Kayla hated being here in the hospital where they kept coming in, but she enjoyed the time she spent talking with Joe.

He rose, walked to the doorway, and smiled. "I'll let you rest now, but I'll be back after I get a bite to eat. If they keep you overnight, the legislature will be in session tomorrow, but I can come around noon."

True to his promise, he came back later with three books, one by each author she'd mentioned. He'd changed into a soft T-shirt, which showed off his muscled arms. How she'd like to be enfolded in them again. "How are you feeling?"

"My arm is much better now." She offered him some chocolates and explained the doctor wouldn't let her drive all the way back to Dallas. "He'll release me, but only if I have someone to stay with me."

Joe grinned. "In that case, I'd be honored to have

125

you as my guest in the Austin apartment I've rented. It's small, but you can have my bed, and I'll sleep on the couch."

"I hate to put you out," she said, but this would be much better than staying with her father. And here, no one would notice they were together. However, she didn't feel up to anything more than sleeping alone in his bed. But spending the whole evening with him would be wonderful.

He was looking at her with a question on his face.

"Yes, I'd love that. It must be expensive to pay for lodging in Dallas and Austin."

"Since the legislature only meets every other year and usually only until June or July, I rented a small apartment. I spend most of my time in Dallas because I work there and because I like to keep an eye on my father, who has Alzheimer's disease. I help my mother out with the things he used to do. My brother and sister aren't much help."

That must take a lot of his time. She admired him for that. "It's too bad he has dementia. I'm sorry you have to deal with that. You're a good son."

He smiled. "I try to be."

They brought the release papers for her to sign and wheeled her to the front door. Joe left to get his car to pick her up.

A few minutes later, as she climbed into the passenger seat, he said, "I'll take you to the Outback restaurant tomorrow for that steak dinner I owe you."

Right now, she felt weak as a newborn kitten, but spending a whole day tomorrow with him would be wonderful. However, she didn't want him to get in trouble. "Don't you have to get back to the legislature session?"

He shook his head. "The speaker called for a recess so we can study the three bills coming up for a vote. The one with the most pages is the park extension one."

After parking his car and leading her into his apartment, Joe got her settled in a kitchen chair, asked what toppings she liked, and ordered pizza. "That's something you can eat with your other hand."

He really was thoughtful. She glanced around the small kitchen. Its open window had colorful curtains and looked out onto a park across the street. Children were running around and playing on the swings, slide, and merry-go-round. Their shouts and laughter made her wish she was out in the sunshine, but it was nice being here with Joe.

After the pizza arrived, and they'd eaten their fill, he led her to his bedroom and invited her to sit in a chair. He gave her a T-shirt to sleep in, got out sheets, and changed the bed. He was really being solicitous.

She climbed into his bed. "I hate to take over your bed."

"I'd rather share it with you." He grinned. "But you need to rest."

Thoughts of being in his arms warmed her heart. Would she feel up to that tomorrow? As bad as she must look, would he even be interested?

He leaned over and kissed her, and oh, what a kiss. His lips roved over her mouth. She met him, kiss for kiss. Somehow, the aches subsided, and all she could think of was lying in his arms. He caressed her uninjured shoulder. She wished he'd fondle her breasts. They ached for his touch. They swelled in anticipation, but he didn't touch her there or lower down.

She smiled. "Somehow, your kisses take me to another place, a wonderful one I don't want to leave."

He beamed. "I can't wait until you're better and we can be together."

"Me, too, but I need to get back to Dallas and my job."

"You must be garnering a lot of attention after winning that sinkhole case against my client."

"I received several congratulations from members of my firm. However, I have to admit you fought valiantly for your client. You came up with more causation scenarios than I could think of."

He nodded. "I tried, but obviously you put up a better case because the jury agreed with you. Now, where's that cream you're supposed to spread on your arm?"

She pointed to where she'd laid it on the bedside table.

He took it and very carefully applied it to her arm. After pulling the sheet up to her neck, but being careful not to cover her burned arm, he kissed her forehead. "Pleasant dreams. I hope you'll feel better tomorrow."

Remembering his adoring smile, she soon fell asleep.

The next day, her arm still hurt, but Kayla was feeling much better. He cooked scrambled eggs and bacon and wouldn't let her help clean up. It felt good to be taken care of like this.

He glanced back at her while washing dishes. "Are you up to a trip to the Arboretum? It's Austin's upscale shopping center. There's an Outback restaurant there. If you feel like it, we can stroll through the Wildflower Center after our steak dinner."

"I'd like that."

They set out in his car, and twenty minutes later, a hostess seated them in the restaurant. They each had a delicious rib eye steak and baked potato with all the trimmings. After lunch, she and Joe wandered through the Lady Bird Wildflower Center. For an hour, they walked past chocolate daisies, lavender-hued asters, and other flowers. As Kayla rose up from smelling a cluster of pink flowers, her neck prickled. "I know it's ridiculous, but I feel like I'm being watched."

Joe shook his head. "It's not likely. No one knows where we are."

Kayla strolled with Joe back to his car. "Now, after taking the pain pills, I feel much better, well enough to drive home. Would you please take me to where I parked my car yesterday? I need to get back to Dallas."

After he parked beside her Toyota, she got out, inhaled the smell of freshly mowed grass, and slid behind the wheel of her car.

Joe stood beside her open window. "Are you sure you feel up to driving back tonight? Why don't you stay with me another day?"

"I'd love to, but I don't want to take advantage of your hospitality any more. Before I go, I want to pick up a hamburger and a milkshake at one of those drive-in fast-food places. Why don't you join me?"

"The sun is setting. Don't you want to head for home while it's still light?"

She shook her head. "It will be dark by the time I get very far, and my mouth is already watering for a milkshake."

Joe smiled. "Well, in that case, let me treat you. I've discovered a place on the edge of town that makes great shakes. We can go in your car, and afterward, you can drop me off back here at my car. By then, the traffic won't be so bad, and it won't take long to drive across town." He climbed into the passenger seat beside her.

She parked near the small glass-and-brick building, and they placed their order. A server brought them each a hamburger and a fudge milkshake. In between sips of his shake, Joe entertained her with interesting comments about people he'd met in the legislature. A gentle breeze wafted in through the open windows.

She finished her shake while he was drinking the last of his. "Give me your cup when you're finished, and I'll throw both away." She opened her car door.

"No. I'll take them." He opened his door. "Just a minute," he said as he drew in the last swallow. "What the—"

A man wearing a ski mask was pulling Joe out the other door. Shocked, Kayla grabbed her phone to call for help, but someone grasped her left arm—thank goodness, not the burned one—and yanked her from her seat.

"Hey. Let go of me," she yelled, struggling to get her feet firmly on the pavement.

"You're coming with us," her assailant said. He wore a bandana around his nose and mouth.

"Help! Someone call the poli—"

The wiry, dark-haired man clapped a hand over her mouth. She struggled to breathe as he dragged her away from her car. The other man, big and burly, was trying to pull Joe back toward the trees at the edge of the property.

She fought the man holding her. Tried to run, but he yanked her wrists behind her. He bent one arm up behind her back until it hurt so badly, she stopped fighting. He looped a rope around her wrists, pulling on the burned arm, making it hurt more.

Kayla gasped. "My arm is burned. Please stop. That hurts so much."

"Hey," her captor asked the other guy, "okay to tie them in front?"

The other man nodded. The first guy spun her around. His body odor washed over her. He bound her hands in front of her. Turned her again. Grabbed her upper arms and pushed her toward a van.

"Help!" she screamed.

He slapped her face. "Shut up, bitch."

In front of the van, she planted her feet. "I'm not getting in."

"Yes, you are." The back door stood open. He lifted her. Dumped her onto the back seat. Slammed the door.

She gasped. Her pulse racing, she sat up and put her feet down. Fast-food containers crunched under her feet.

She reached for the handle. It wouldn't release. Must be a child-resistant lock. "Help," she screamed, but the windows were closed. No one could hear.

The two men shoved Joe in beside her from the other side. His head hit her thigh. They'd tied his hands behind him. She leaned back over him. Tried to stretch her arm to reach the handle, but couldn't reach it. It was probably locked also, damn it. The stocky guy was behind the wheel, and the van was moving.

Joe sat up. "How did they get the jump on us? Damn it. I should have been more aware. Should have protected you."

"Did they take your wallet?"

He nodded. "I still have my legislator's name badge on. Probably think I'm loaded."

Kayla's thoughts raced. "What do you want with us?" she asked their abductors.

The wiry guy peered over the back of the passenger seat. "You're good-looking enough—"

They might have taken Joe's money, but that other guy had different ideas. Her teeth chattered. She shrunk in her seat. Tried working at her wrist ties with her teeth.

"Hey, knock it off, Bill," the driver said. "She's just along for the ride. Keep your mind on our goal."

"Okay, but you're going ten miles over the speed limit. Better slow down. Might be a cop nearby."

"Shut up. I'm watching."

Joe whispered to Kayla, "Hope one does…show up."

"We can't be that lucky." She twisted her neck to look back.

A siren sounded. Far behind them, an SUV with lights flashing raced toward them. Kayla let out the breath she'd been holding. "Maybe help's on the way."

"Phil, don't cha hear the siren? There's a cop coming behind us."

"I am slowing down," he snapped.

The siren came closer. Flashing lights sent red and blue streaks into the van.

The police car raced past them and kept going.

"Damn," Joe muttered. He squeezed Kayla's hand and laid his head back against the seat.

Disappointed, Kayla let her chin sink to her chest.

"Whew, that was close," Phil said.

"Better keep under the speed limit," said his partner. "Might be another one near."

"Hell, Bill, I know that. I'm not stupid."

"Hold out your hands," Joe whispered. "I'll get them

free." He fiddled with them for a moment. "Damn it. I can't undo them."

"Turn your back to me," she whispered. "I'll untie you." She tried to undo his knot, but it was too tight. Finally, she gave up and whispered in his ear, "I can't get you loose."

"Hey, Phil," the wiry guy in the passenger seat said. "They're plotting to escape. We gotta do something about that."

"Open the glove compartment and get out the plastic bag."

Chapter Ten

A moment later, Phil pulled over to the shoulder, parked the van, and got out.

The door on Joe's side opened. Phil reached in and pulled Joe away from her. Joe struggled as Kayla tried to push Phil away. Phil grabbed Joe and stabbed a syringe in his neck.

Then he reached for Kayla.

Joe scowled at Phil. "Leave her alon—" He moaned and collapsed against the back of the seat.

Oh, no. Kayla gasped. Was Joe still breathing?

Chills ran down her back. She leaned as far away as she could. "Don't," she said, but Phil grabbed her.

He injected her. The men both climbed back in front. Phil pulled onto the highway and accelerated.

Feeling woozy, Kayla leaned against Joe, and darkness took her.

****

Sometime later, not sure how long she'd been out, Kayla came to. It was dark, and they were still in that gray van. It was cruising down an exit road. Joe had his eyes open. "Do you know where we are?" she whispered.

Joe shrugged. "I have no idea, but before I passed out, we were heading north." He sat upright, facing the front window. "I didn't catch the name of the road on the last exit sign."

Now they traveled over a two-lane, asphalt road through mostly treeless countryside. They passed an occasional house.

In the distance, a siren sounded. Someone turned on the radio. Static sounded, then an annoying loud buzz. "This is a tornado warning for Collin County. A funnel was spotted two miles east of Gunter."

"That means we're north of Dallas," Kayla whispered.

Phil's head swiveled. "Do you see a funnel anywhere?"

Bill shook his head. "Shit no. It's dark out. How far is Gunter from here?"

"Three miles. Damn. Need to stash them and get the hell away from here." He sped up.

Kayla gasped. He'd said *stash*. Were they going to leave them tied up somewhere?

Ten minutes later, he turned onto another road.

The sound of the tires on gravel grated on Kayla's ears. The van made another turn. She rose up to see out the front window. Trees and underbrush lined both sides of the road. The bumpy ride hinted the road was lined with ruts. After driving a way, Phil stopped the van and got out.

Trees hung over the road. They were in the middle of nowhere.

Were they going to kill her and Joe and leave their bodies here? She swallowed a lump in her throat.

Squeaks sounded. Phil was opening a gate. He got back in the van, drove about ten yards, and stopped in front of a log cabin. Peeling paint tarnished the front door. A thin swath of weeds separated the cabin from the surrounding woods.

Bill opened the door on her side. "Get out."

Knee-high weeds framed a narrow dirt path. Bill stood there, ready to grab her if she tried to run. She could try, but she didn't know where they were. The dense woods around the cabin looked foreboding. Swollen, dark clouds loomed overhead. Lightning flashed, and thunder rumbled. In the distance, a howl sounded, maybe a coyote.

Bill pushed her toward the house. Ahead of her, Phil was trying to shove Joe through the open doorway, but he was resisting. Rain fell, dampening Kayla's skin.

Bill grabbed Kayla's arm and shoved her toward the open door. The rain came down harder, soaking her hair and her clothes. After Phil managed to push Joe inside, Bill shoved her through the doorway. She caught her foot on the doorjamb and fell onto the linoleum. Quickly, he tied her ankles together.

Bill tried to bind Joe's ankles, but Joe kicked him. Finally, Phil, big and burly, got Joe down on the floor, sat on his legs, and tied his ankles. Phil walked into another room. She heard drawers being opened and shut. He returned, a butcher knife clutched in his hand.

Kayla gasped. Edged toward the door. Was he going to stab them?

Bill looked alarmed. "Hey, I don't want to be part of any killing."

"We weren't hired for that, but I'm not leaving this here so they can cut themselves loose."

Bill beckoned to Phil. "How close is this cabin to where a tornado was sighted?"

"Too damn close. I don't want to be anywhere near there. Now we've got those two stashed, I'm heading for I-75. Come on." He hurried outside. Bill followed. As the door slammed behind him, his words were audible. "Now he won't be sitting in Austin—"

The cold, hard floor pushed against Kayla's hip. "What's he talking about?" she asked. The driver was gunning the van's motor. Tires crunched on the hard dirt road as they left. Lightning flashed, followed quickly by a loud clap of thunder.

Joe shrugged. "Guess they don't want me to go back to the legislature." He sat up. "See anything around we could use to saw the ropes?"

Kayla rose up on her knees. "There could be another knife in the kitchen."

Lightning flashed again. A tremendous clap of thunder followed. Rain pounded against the windows. "Maybe we better move to a safer part of this cabin," Joe said. He inclined his head toward a doorway. "I saw cots in the bedroom, but we should be safer in the bathroom. Let's get in there. Then we can worry about untying ourselves."

It seemed to take forever to inch there with her ankles tied together, but finally, Kayla managed to follow Joe into the small bathroom. A tremendous clap of thunder sounded. Pounding rain sounded even louder in the bathroom. Outside, branches or twigs from a large bush scraped against the house. At least the window was small and high up. Less likely they'd get hit by broken glass.

She rose up on her knees and reached for the light switch. Her fingers finally closed over it, but when she pushed it, nothing happened. "Great, the electricity must be off, but I had better close the door." She stood and pushed it shut using her back. The noise of the storm didn't let up. The thunder got louder.

"Sit down and face me," Joe said. "I'll try to untie your wrists."

Finally, the rope around her wrists fell away. "Thanks," she said.

"How's your burned arm feel now?"

"My skin is raw, but it feels good to move my arms." She stuck her legs out and pulled one foot loose from her shoe. She slipped her other foot out and untied her ankles.

Lightning flashed, and darkness returned. "You know," Joe said, "even tied up, you are one good-looking woman. And I like that you never panicked or gave up."

That made her smile despite their situation.

"Hey," he said, "aren't you going to try to untie me?"

"Sure." She knelt behind him, cold tile floor pressing against her knees. She pulled at the knotted cords around his wrists. Finally, she got one loop free and untied his hands.

"Thanks. I'll get my feet free."

After a minute, he pulled the cord loose and stuck out one leg beside the toilet. "There's not much room to stretch out here."

The scratching on the window continued, accompanied by the patter of rain. The wind whistled, and the rain came down harder.

Another loud clap of thunder sounded. Kayla cringed. "I think we'd better stay in the bathroom," Kayla said.

A loud crash sounded.

"What was that?" she asked.

"Maybe a tree fell on the roof." He pulled the door open a crack and gazed out into the living room. "The ceiling's leaking."

"There should be a basin under that." She rose up to go look for one. "That's silly. Why am I worrying about this dilapidated cabin?"

Kayla sat back down behind Joe. "We may be here for quite a while. I'm scared. Talk to me. It will take my mind off thinking about what a tornado could do to this cabin. What was it like growing up in your family?"

"When I was in high school, we moved to Coppell. My parents still live there." He explained about his father's Alzheimer's slowly getting worse. "I need to be there for my dad and my mother. My brother and sister don't help much."

"Oh, that's too bad. That must be hard to deal with."

"Dad was fine while we were growing up. Took my brother, Diego, and me fishing several times and—"

A sudden roar sounding like a train drowned out his words. Sent fear through Kayla. She gasped, wrapped her arms around Joe's waist. Put her head on his shoulder. She clung to him. "I've never been so scared in all my life." Warmth from his body comforted her, but her heart was beating fast. She gasped in quick breaths.

He put his face next to hers so she could hear him over the blast. "You just got out of the hospital. I hate having you dragged into this because of me. The last time I was this scared, I was six. It was even scarier than this because now I have you to share it with."

"What happened?"

"I went on a hike with my father and brother. I ran on up ahead to check on a noise. Thought it was a wolf. The next thing I knew, I couldn't see Dad or Diego. I'd left the path and couldn't remember exactly how I'd got there. I wasn't sure which way to go. I hollered, 'Dad,' but no one answered. I was afraid I'd have to spend the night in the woods with who knew what wild animals that might attack me."

"I bet you were terrified."

"You'd better believe it. I kept yelling and looking around."

"How long before they found you?"

"It seemed like forever, but when Dad and Diego found me, Dad said they'd been looking for half an hour."

"I bet that was the last time you ran off so far from people you were with."

He nodded. The noise got deafening. Breathing fast, she checked the luminous numbers on her watch and noted the time. How long did tornado blasts last? Finally, after what seemed like an eternity but was only eight minutes, the noise lessened. The funnel must have moved farther away.

Finally, all she heard were the sounds of the rain splattering against the small, high window. "Do you think it's safe to open the door?"

"Let's wait a few minutes."

The sky lightened. His hand caressed her cheek, drawing her attention from the window. "At least I'm alone with an attractive, capable woman, one who can chew my ass in court."

That made her smile. She grinned at his comment about her actions in court. Leaning against his chest, she felt comforted by his touch. She could feel his heart beating against her hand. "I feel much safer being here with you."

"Since we're not active adversaries in court…" He cradled her chin with his hands. His face moved closer…

His breaths warmed her cheeks. He hesitated a few seconds as if assessing her willingness.

Yes, she wanted to kiss him. Filled with anticipation, she inched close and waited. His lips moved closer, and he gently tasted hers. His mouth was warm and welcome. She liked the way it felt against hers. She leaned in and responded. This was nice, better than nice. He was a great kisser.

He deepened the kiss, roving and tasting, then dipped his tongue between her lips. She let her tongue tangle with his, enjoying the way it slid over the inside of her mouth while the wind howled outside.

His hands found her breasts, caressing and squeezing. He set her on fire. Her nipples firmed. He unbuttoned her blouse, took one in his mouth, and suckled it through her lace bra. She surged toward him. Thunder rolled as longing for more energized her entire body. "Oh, Joe."

With a sudden blast of wind, the door opened and pushed against Kayla's back. Damn. Did the storm have to spoil everything? "Move. I need to shut the door." She backed away from him in the cramped space. She shoved the door with all her strength. Couldn't close it.

He stood. "Let me get it." Another thunderous boom sounded.

Together, they wrestled with the door. Fought the wind as it pushed the door against them. They strained harder. Icy wind rippled her sleeve. Chilled her flesh. A wide crack opened between the door and the living room.

It was dark, but lightning revealed broken glass littering the floor. Rain blew in the holes. Wind had strewn sticks, stones, and leafy twigs about. With every breath came the smell of dirt and rain. A chair clattered across the floor. Her pulse raced. Would the wind blast debris through the bathroom doorway to pummel them? She placed her shoulder against the door and shoved as hard as she could. So did Joe. It seemed to be a losing battle.

"Push harder," she yelled.

Joe leaned against the door, putting his shoulder against it. They both shoved. Finally got it shut. "Lock it," Joe said.

The storm blew the door inward again. She moved up to help him push. They finally got it shut again. Darkness closed over them.

Kayla grabbed the small lever. "Can't lock it."

"Move. Let me do it," Joe said. Joe pushed her fingers away. The knob clicked, and the door held. "Now, we wait."

The storm's roar continued. The closed door lessened the wind's noise, but sounds of debris and glass crashing on the living room floor kept up. So did the pounding rain.

Joe leaned against the door. He reached for her hands. "Come closer."

She moved over next to him. He put his arms around her and pulled her against his firm chest, warming her despite her wet shirt.

He spoke in her ear. "We're going to be okay. We can wait it out."

With him holding her tight, she believed him. And as he spoke, the roar abated. Branches brushed against the small window.

Then it was still except for the rain coming down.

"Wow. I never appreciated quiet so much before," she said.

"Me neither." Joe pressed a soft kiss on her lips and gave her a squeeze.

But that wasn't enough. She clasped her hands behind his neck and kissed him. She enjoyed the feel of his mouth against hers and the way he prolonged the kiss until she had to break away to catch her breath.

He caressed her shoulder. "Let's get out of here." He stood and pulled the door open.

She missed the warmth and the safe feeling he'd given her. She stepped closer as lightning flashed. "Oh, my. What a mess."

He shoved aside a chair blocking the doorway and stepped out. Kayla stood in the doorway. In addition to the broken glass and twigs, pieces of wood and what looked like part of a truck's front bumper lay strewn on the floor. What she couldn't see might even look worse.

"Watch where you step. I don't want you to get hurt. Here's a chair you can sit on." He brushed it off. "As I remember, there's another one around somewhere. I'll see if I can find it."

He reached out for a moment. "There it is." He dragged it upright and sat next to her. "Those guys might try to come back when the weather calms down. We need to get out of here and back to civilization."

"As a teenager, I once went to a church camp near Gunter. If we can hike to the gravel road, I might see something that looks familiar. And we might be able to flag down a car. The road probably goes to Gunter."

Lightning flashed twice in quick succession, now revealing a tree, which had fallen through the porch roof. A tangle of branches blocked the doorway.

Kayla stared through the darkness. She gasped. "Oh, my gosh. How are we going to get out of here? I didn't see a back door in the kitchen, and the bathroom window's too small to climb out."

"I don't think we should try anything tonight. If those men return, hopefully that tree will hold them back. I need to get to Austin by tomorrow's afternoon vote, but it's too dark to crawl out of here safely. Let's start out first thing tomorrow morning."

She nodded. "Even if we could get past the tree, we don't want to risk an injury that might slow us down. We'd better stay here tonight."

"You're right. Thank goodness, the rain has stopped, and the moon has risen. We should be able to find our way to those cots."

"Do you know why they kidnapped us and left us here?" she asked.

He rubbed his neck. "Well, I can't vote for the park bill, which is scheduled for a vote tomorrow. I've spoken publicly in favor of it. Maybe someone wants to stop me from voting." He frowned. "My developer client is against it. He wants to build on that land."

Kayla thought a moment. "My client asked me to tell my father to vote against it, but I refused. Do you think he will?"

"I think your dad's in favor of it. At least he'll be there to vote." Joe glanced around at their surroundings. "This cabin is a dump, but at least I'm alone with an amazing, brave woman. You haven't complained, and I couldn't ask for a better woman to be abducted with." A flash of lightning revealed Joe's grin, which cheered her.

Stumbling through the darkness, she kicked some debris aside and finally made her way to the bedroom with two cots. She sank down on a lumpy mattress. "Well, at least this is better than the floor."

"Hey, there's a window in here. Maybe we can get out that way." Joe stepped over to the window. Light from the moon silhouetted a big, thick, trash tree standing on the other side of the window, blocking their way. "Damn, why would someone plant a tree in front of a window?"

"A seed probably took hold and grew. I'm guessing the place has been mostly deserted."

Moonlight shone through the window. It cast a swath on his broad chest and muscular arms, tempting her. He sat on the opposite cot. "Sorry, I can't offer you better accommodations."

Kayla laughed. "And this time, I'll be sleeping with you without touching you."

He took a deep breath. "I enjoyed being with you that night—a lot—but maybe we'd better get some sleep." He glanced around the dreary room, his face a study in disappointment. "Maybe sometime later, we can be together where it's nice. Those men may still come back. As soon as it's daylight, we'd better see if we can head out. 'Til then, pleasant dreams."

Pleasant dreams, yeah, right. She hoped she wouldn't dream of the kidnapping and the tornado. A good night kiss would have been nice. Although they were still on opposite sides of a divorce case, she felt even more drawn to him. Memories of that first night made her want to be close to him again, skin to skin, and make love with him.

She walked over and sat beside him on the cot. "How about a good night kiss so I'll have pleasant dreams instead of nightmares about those men?"

He took her hand but didn't move closer. "I don't trust myself to take you in my arms and stop there, but I won't deny you a kiss." He leaned toward her. The kiss, sweeter than apple cider, was too short.

She moved closer, took hold of his shoulders, and kissed him. Sliding her hands around his neck, feeling the firm skin and crisp hairs, she kissed with all the pent-up feeling he inspired. He pulled her tight against his firm chest. His hands grasped her shoulders, sending warmth and anticipation through her body.

Without breaking their kiss, he caressed both her breasts. Her entire body quivered with excitement.

Being next to him felt so good. Still caressing her breasts, he kissed her again, a long, lingering kiss, so satisfying she didn't even want to break to catch a breath.

Joe backed off an inch to whisper. "What if those guys come back? Do you want to take the chance?" He grasped her waist. "I love being together with you, but it's your choice."

He was a gentleman through and through. She admired him for that.

His kisses enthralled her, and his caresses excited her. She nestled herself against him, enfolding herself in the warmth of his body. "Yes, Counselor, I want more. I want all of you."

He nodded. "Counselor, I accept your proposition." He slid his hand between them, undid another button on her blouse, then paused. "I, uh, have no protection."

"Don't worry. I'm on the pill, and as far as anything else, I trust you are clean and healthy as I am." She leaned back a little and unfastened his shirt buttons.

As soon as they were undressed, Joe pulled her onto the cot. She grabbed a blanket to cover their bodies.

He kissed her forehead. "We won't need that. I'll keep you warm." His mouth covered hers for a long searching kiss. She cradled his face in her hands and kissed him back for all she was worth.

When they finally broke the kiss, Joe raised his chest. "You look beautiful in the moonlight, all curves and shadows."

She smiled and wished she could see his face better.

He caressed her shoulders and kissed her neck. He smoothed his hands over her shoulders and slid them down to her breasts. As he squeezed them, she thrilled with anticipation. If those men didn't come back and break their way into the front room, there might be time to enjoy each other tonight.

Joe suckled one bare breast, setting off a fire inside her. When he moved to her other breast, the flames grew higher. Full of wonder, she knew it would get even better as the night wore on.

She pulled his face down for a kiss. "You're lighting fires inside me."

He pulled her hand down to his shaft. "You could make me hotter."

She loved touching him and feeling him grow bigger and stiffer.

He smiled. "Let me pleasure you."

She liked the way he thought of her enjoyment and didn't just concentrate on his own. Already, his warm fingers were teasing her folds, which were damp by now. He found her nub. Stroked it with his thumb. His touch set excitement coursing through her body. When he slid a finger inside, tingles escalated. The feelings kept getting stronger until an orgasm, stronger than she'd ever felt before, struck her full force. She hugged him tighter. "Being with you like this is wonderful. I want you inside me now."

Moonlight from the window lit up his grin. "Your wish is my command."

He was hard and ready for her.

He kissed her again.

Wrapping her legs and arms around him, she reveled in his thrusts and pushed back with equal force. Her body felt alive, ready to keep going as long as she wanted. She kissed him. "I love the way you make me feel. Oh, my gosh, you're sending me to the stars. Come with me."

The tingles started again. They kept building and building. Could they go any higher? Excited, she pushed against his thrusts, hugging him tightly and kissing him again.

The pulsing reached a crescendo, making her heart sing. His release mingled with hers. She snuggled against him, hoping he felt as fulfilled as she did.

Even though they were in a dangerous situation— those men might come back—she wanted to feel this way forever.

Could she be falling in love with him?

He kissed her and rolled to her side. "This was all I've been dreaming about since the first time we made love. If I weren't so tired, I'd ask for an encore. We might as well stay close to keep warm, but we'd better get dressed just in case those men come back."

And true to his word, after they dressed, he held her in his arms until she fell asleep.

In the morning, she awakened first and touched his arm. He was sleeping soundly, so she shook his upper arm, marveling at the powerful muscle under her fingers. "Wake up. We need to get out of here."

He sat up. "You're right. How's your arm? Is it feeling any better?"

"It doesn't hurt as much as it did. Let's see what we can do about that downed tree." She stepped over broken glass and debris and pushed at the branch. It didn't budge.

Joe walked over beside her and pointed to a thicker branch below. "This is what we need to concentrate our efforts on." He grabbed hold of it. "Put your hands above mine."

After she did, he said, "Now, give it your best try."

She pushed as hard as she could, but they only moved it a few inches.

Joe glanced at the door. "We need to move it at least a foot. Let's try again."

She helped him shove, but it didn't move much.

Joe faced her. "We need to try harder."

She grabbed the trunk again, feeling the rough bark against her hands, and shoved hard until the tree scraped across the porch floor and away from the doorway.

Joe hugged her. "We did it. Now let's get out of here."

Outside, a layer of golden sky heralded the imminent rising of the sun. Unseen birds chirped nearby. She trod beside him. After reaching the gravel road, she wished she'd worn thicker-soled shoes. Each stone pressed against the soles of her feet as she walked. On the dirt road, she took care not to step in any muddy ruts.

Joe pointed to some weeds pulled up by the roots. "Is that poison ivy?"

Kayla shook her head. "It's Virginia creeper."

"Sort of reminds me of marijuana," he said.

"That doesn't look anything like weed...omigosh. Thad Thayer wanted to grow it in that land where the park extension would be. If he was planning to harvest a lot of marijuana, he might be behind the men who kidnapped us so you wouldn't vote for the park extension."

Oh, no. She turned her face away from Joe. "I shouldn't have told you that. I'm betraying client confidentiality."

"Well, under the circumstances, I'm glad you did. I didn't put two and two together until now. And it was his restaurant where I ate lunch and got poisoned."

Joe scowled. "All this time I've been blaming my client for our predicament when it might be your client who's trying to keep me from voting in Austin."

"What my client does that I don't know about isn't my fault."

Joe didn't say another word.

The occasional breeze sent a chill through her sleeves. Joe hailed the first pickup that came along, which was going the wrong way.

She frowned. "Why stop him? We need to go in the other direction."

"We can ask how far it is to town."

The driver stopped.

"We've been kidnapped but finally got away," Joe said. "We need to contact the police. How far is it to town?"

"Oh, that's awful. It's about three miles, give or take, to town. Do you want to use my phone to call the cops? I've got the number in contacts."

"Thanks. I'd appreciate that."

After the man found the number and handed over his phone, Joe called the local police, explained what happened, and gave a description of Phil and Bill. "No, I don't have time to stop in at the station. As a member of the Texas House, I need to get to Austin to vote on a bill. However, I'll be sure to let the Austin police know because those men took us captive there."

He handed the phone back. "Thanks for letting me use that." He looked at Kayla. "Are you up to walking to the next town, or do you want to wait and see if any other cars come by?"

"We might as well start walking."

"Ah, shucks," the driver said, "get in. I'm not in a hurry, and that isn't much out of my way."

Glad to rest her feet, Kayla climbed in. Joe sat beside her. They passed a house with the roof mostly blown off and another with all the windows broken. It looked deserted, thank goodness. "We must have been right on the tornado's path," Joe said.

"We were lucky we didn't get hurt," she said.

The driver went uphill and downhill and around curves in the road. Crows cawed, and a hawk circled, probably hunting some small creature to eat.

****

Finally, they reached a convenience store on the edge of town. Joe and Kayla got out. Joe thanked the driver, and he drove off.

Joe rubbed his chin and looked at Kayla. "For all we know, my ex-client and yours might be working together to keep the park extension from happening."

After they walked inside the convenience store, the proprietor agreed to let them use the phone. After several tries, Joe connected with an Uber driver who agreed to take them to Dallas. While they waited for the driver, Kayla asked, "What will happen if you are not there when the park extension comes up for a vote? Do you really think the bill will be defeated if you are not there?"

Joe nodded. "From what I can tell, the number of favorable members is about equal to the number opposed. However, I can ask a friend to cast a vote for me if I'm absent."

"How can he do that?"

"He can step over to my desk and push the button marked 'Aye.' They call that ghost voting, but it's allowed if I ask him to cast a vote for me. Could be why the kidnappers took our phones, but maybe I can call in a vote." He turned to the store clerk. "May I use your phone again?"

After the clerk nodded, Joe punched in some numbers. "He'd better answer. His number is the only one I remember." Joe held the phone to his ear. It rang and rang. Joe left a message to call right back. He got another representative's number from Information, but he didn't answer either. Joe waited five minutes, but the Uber driver came. "Damn, we have to leave now."

After Joe followed Kayla into the back seat, the driver headed for the freeway. Joe faced Kayla. "I really need to get there in time to vote. There's been a lot of opposition to that bill. One of my legislator friends may not vote. Someone threatened him with disclosure of some information he doesn't want public. I suggested he contact the police to charge the man."

"Do you think he will?"

"I don't know. With a close vote, a representative may call for a record vote."

"What's that mean?"

"If any member calls for a vote of ayes and nays and one-fifth of those present agree, members must take a record vote. Instead of members saying aye or nay, each legislator must push the aye or nay button to record the vote electronically, but my friend doesn't want his vote to be public information."

"Because then the blackmailer will find out how your friend voted."

Joe nodded.

"How are you going to get to Austin in time?" Kayla asked.

"I'll fly. I've got an old truck I can drive to the airport." Needing to get to Dallas quickly, Joe resented the time it took the driver to get them to his house.

After the driver parked at his house, Joe authorized a tip for him, then asked how much extra it would cost to drive Kayla to her apartment.

She shook her head. "Never mind that. I'm coming with you. I want to see that bill passed. I'll pay for my ticket, and besides, my car is in Austin."

Joe stared at her. "You sure are passionate about that park extension. Okay, let me get some ID, book our flights, and pick up the keys to my truck. We'll have to pick up some ID at your place." He held the door open for her.

Minutes later, he backed the truck out of the garage. "Your chariot awaits."

Kayla climbed in, and Joe drove off.

After a quick trip to her apartment for her passport to use as ID, Joe headed for the airport and parked. Once inside, Joe used a public phone to call David Walker. "When will the vote be held?"

"This afternoon about three o'clock."

"I'm flying in from Dallas, but I should get there this afternoon."

"You'd better call your mother," David said. "Your father's in the hospital."

Joe sighed. "Thanks for letting me know. I'll call my mother. If his condition is serious, I won't get there in time for the vote."

Joe called his mom. He could hardly understand her because she was crying. "Mom, just calm down and tell me what's happened to Dad."

"I've been trying to call you all morning, but you didn't answer."

"I didn't have my phone with me, but never mind that. Tell me about Dad." He held his breath and listened.

"Your father is in intensive care at Parkland Hospital. They said he had a heart attack."

"How bad was it? Is he going to survive?"

"They won't say. The doctor said they'd do what they could, but he wasn't sure. You'd better get here as soon as possible."

After swallowing a gasp, Joe said goodbye and beckoned Kayla over.

As he told her what he'd learned, Joe's heart twisted. It was bad enough his father was slowly losing his memory, but his father might not survive a heart attack. Joe swallowed. He wasn't ready for his father to disappear from his life.

Chapter Eleven

Joe cancelled their flights and hurried with Kayla back to his truck. He headed for Parkland.

Up ahead, an eighteen-wheeler was hogging the street in front of them. Joe frowned. "That damn truck stays just under the speed limit. I'm going to pass it." He sped up. It took a long time to pass it. He gunned the motor for more speed and didn't slow down until they were way in front of the truck.

A siren sounded. A police car, flashing red and blue lights, zoomed round the truck.

Joe scowled. "Damn. That's all I need to ruin my day."

"Better pull over," Kayla said. "Hope this doesn't take too long."

He drove the car onto the shoulder and eased to a stop. The damn truck rolled on by, and the police car parked behind them.

Joe rolled the window down, then kept his hands on the wheel. "I don't know why we got stopped. I wasn't going that fast. She'd better not delay us very long, or I may not get to see my father before he dies. When I tell him why I don't have my driver's license, I hope he believes me."

The officer, a hefty, middle-aged woman in a dark-blue uniform with a shoulder patch saying "Dallas Police," walked up to the window.

"Do you know you were going six miles over the speed limit? May I see your driver's license, please?"

"I didn't realize I was going that fast. I was trying to pass that eighteen-wheeler. It was going just under the speed limit. My father just had a heart attack, and I need to get to the hospital."

"Passing is no excuse for going over the speed limit. Now, let me see your driver's license."

"I don't have it with me, but I can give you the number." Joe recited it.

The officer frowned. "I'll check it out. Do you have your registration and proof of insurance?"

"Kayla, would you look in the glove compartment for that, please?"

She searched through the maps and papers, then pulled out a slip of paper, and handed it to Joe. He held it out the window.

The officer studied the form. "Are you the owner of the truck?"

Joe nodded, took a deep breath, and huffed it out. He tapped his fingers on his knee, wishing the officer would hurry things up.

"What's your name and address?" asked the officer as she scrutinized the document.

Joe recited the facts, hoping the registration wasn't out of date. It couldn't be that long since he'd paid for it.

The officer handed the slip back. "I'm issuing you a ticket. If you can produce a valid license in court, that charge will be dismissed, but you'll still be charged for speeding." She held out a narrow slip and a pen. "Please sign here."

It was hard to write, using the rough surface of the center of the wheel, but he finally managed, then handed the paper out the window.

The officer tore off a carbon copy and handed him the ticket. "Instructions about when to pay the ticket or protest it in court are printed on the ticket. See that you comply."

"May I leave now?"

"Yes, but see that you follow the speed limit. That keeps everyone safe. Have a good day." She headed back to her cruiser.

"Damn it all anyhow," Joe muttered as he pulled onto the road, taking care to keep under the speed limit.

Kayla didn't say a word, but she looked tense. Keeping his eye on the speedometer, he said a silent prayer for his dad.

He gripped the wheel and hoped his dad would pull through and not die before they got there.

"I'll come in the hospital with you," Kayla said.

"I'm not sure how my father will respond to you. He's got Alzheimer's."

Kayla reached out to touch his arm. "Oh, that's right."

"My mother, bless her heart, thinks he's just forgetful. She hasn't taken him to the doctor about that. I'm really worried. I hate to think the man who read me stories at bedtime, helped me go over spelling words before tests, and took me fishing won't remember any of that."

"Sounds like he was a good father to you."

Joe nodded. "I hope he keeps on recognizing me."

"Surely he will. If not, that's too awful to contemplate."

"Right now, I hope he survives his heart attack."

Finally, the sign for Parkland showed up, but Joe

had to deal with a traffic jam. He found a spot and parked the truck.

****

After Kayla stepped out, Joe walked around the back of the truck and took hold of her hand. "You've been a great sport." He pulled her to him and kissed her. His lips were warm and expressive. It seemed as if he couldn't get enough of her. "Let's go in. I need to see my father."

Her lips were still tingling from his kiss as Kayla hurried to keep up with his long strides.

Joe walked through the hospital doors. "I don't know how he'll act, so be prepared."

Five minutes later, after asking directions, they found the right room. Joe rushed in and hugged his mom, then moved to his father's bedside.

Kayla paused at the doorway. Mr. Morales, Sr. lay there with his eyes closed. Joe stood by his father's side, looking concerned. The monitor wasn't visible from the doorway. Hopefully, it wouldn't show a flat line.

She stepped inside. The monitor showed a slightly erratic line, but she didn't know what was normal. The slender, gray-haired lady with a solemn face and bags under her eyes must be Joe's mother.

Joe held out his arm toward Kayla. "Mom, I'd like you to meet my girlfriend, Kayla."

He'd called her his girlfriend. That gave her a warm feeling. Not knowing if he'd told his mother about their abduction, Kayla didn't mention it, but smiled and nodded. "It's nice to meet you. Sorry it's not under better circumstances."

His mother glanced her way. "Do you work in the same office Joe does?"

"No, I work at Brown and Leggitt."

"Joe hasn't mentioned you before. Are you new to the area?"

Kayla smoothed down her pants, hoping they didn't look too rumpled. "I grew up here, but Joe and I went to different high schools."

"So, you went right to work after high school?"

Kayla shook her head. "No, I—"

"She's an attorney, Mom," Joe said.

"Oh, I see. You look awfully young to have finished that much schooling."

"Thank you," Kayla said, but didn't feel like she'd been complimented.

"So, have you and Joe been dating awhile?"

"A few weeks," Kayla said.

"I'm glad he has some friends here," his mom said. "The ones he grew up with have mostly moved away." She turned to face him. "Whatever happened to Ellen? You and she went together in high school. I thought maybe you two were getting serious, but then I haven't seen her around. Has she moved?"

"No, Mother, she's still in town."

Kayla brushed a lock of hair from her face. Ellen was not only still around, but she obviously wanted him back. Joe had introduced Kayla as a girlfriend, and they'd shared a night that was both awful and wonderful beyond measure, but how did he really feel about her?

Mr. Morales opened his eyes. Joe asked, "How are you feeling, Dad?"

"Not good," he mumbled. "I…"

"I hope you'll feel better soon." He beckoned for Kayla to come closer. After she did, Joe said, "Dad, I'd like you to meet my friend, Kayla."

"Hello," his father said in a weak voice. "What's

your name again? Have I met you before?"

"No, but it's nice to meet you," Kayla said. "I'm sorry you're not feeling well."

A pudgy nurse in pink scrubs walked in, took Mr. Morales's blood pressure. "These numbers are pretty high."

Mr. Morales shut his eyes. His arms lay by his side with his fingers relaxed.

The nurse faced the rest of them. "Why don't you let him rest. You can come back later."

"I don't know," his mother said. "Maybe I should stay here with him." She gently touched her husband's forehead. "He doesn't seem to have a fever or be perspiring. I guess it would be okay to leave him for a while."

Joe's mother faced Joe. "Let me take you two to lunch at a nearby restaurant, and we'll let Dad rest for a while." She turned toward Kayla. "If you don't mind, that is."

"Sure," Kayla said.

Joe put his hand on the small of his mother's back. "Come on, Mom. It will be good for you to get out and let him sleep for a while."

A little while later, they were seated in a nearby Jason's Deli. Although the restaurant was crowded with lunch patrons, the redheaded waitress soon brought broccoli cheese soup for his mother and well-stacked Reuben sandwiches for Kayla and Joe.

His mother sipped her soup, then laid down her spoon. "My goodness, those are big sandwiches. Kayla, are you going to eat the whole thing?"

Kayla nodded. "I've had these before. They are delicious, and I probably will eat it all." Kayla tried to swallow the bite of sandwich past the lump in her throat. Would she really want to be invited to dinner at his parents' house? Well, that wasn't likely to happen until Mr. Morales, Sr. got well.

His mother set down her soup spoon. "Joe said you had two cases against each other. Joe's a wonderful attorney. I'm sure he won them both."

Joe shook his head. "Actually, she won the bigger one to the tune of half a million dollars. Our other clients are still wrangling over the final decree."

Mrs. Morales's eyes widened. "That's an outrageous amount. Kayla, you must be a real cutthroat attorney."

Kayla didn't feel like that had been a compliment. A headache pained her temples, but she tried to ignore it. "I work hard to get good settlements for my clients. This one had to pay a lot to fill up the sinkhole and shore up his house."

"Oh, I see," Mrs. Morales said. "No wonder there was such a large settlement."

Joe leaned toward his mother. "Mom, I don't have my phone with me. May I borrow yours for an important call?"

"Sure," his mother said and fished her phone from her purse. Joe reached across the table and laid his hand on Kayla's. "Please excuse me. I need to call your father and find out how the vote went. I'm going to step over to the window." As he stood there talking, Kayla waited, hoping he'd learn the bill had been passed.

His mother leaned closer and spoke in a low voice. "I haven't told Joe yet what else the doctor told me."

Chapter Twelve

Joe clicked the number for the speaker and got a message. David Walker wasn't answering his phone? Joe frowned.

Kayla walked up beside him. "What's the matter?"

He checked his watch. "It's after one. The legislature should be back in session after a lunch break. I'll have to wait until after five." He texted a message to David.

"Are you calling someone else now?" Her tone was all businesslike, but the way she looked at him seemed intense. That made him smile. He had to stop thinking about kissing her.

He shook his head and returned to the table. "I sent a text to Kayla's father, who's Speaker of the House. A lot of representatives were against the bill. If it gets voted down, I need to think of ways to let my constituents know the bill didn't pass."

"Do you have to mention it?" his mother asked. "Maybe your constituents won't notice it. Many people don't read the papers anymore."

"Bad idea. I need to be transparent."

How are you going to announce that?" Kayla asked. "On your website, the paper, the radio?"

"I could do an announcement in neighborhood weekly paper, but how many people actually read those?"

"Why not a town hall meeting?" his mother asked.

That would subject him to vocal questions and angry comments. He frowned. Not something to look forward to. "I wouldn't call one just for that," he said. "I'll probably tell a reporter at *The Dallas Morning News*."

"I'm proud of you," his mother said. "You're a rarity, an honest politician."

His mother picked up the check and handed her credit card to the waiter.

"Thanks for buying us lunch," Joe said. "Kayla, I'm driving Mom and me back to the hospital. Would you like me to take you home or drop you off at your office?"

She looked at her wrinkled pants and blouse. "I'd like to go home and change, but I know you want to get back to your father as soon as possible. Just drop me off at my office."

Joe shook his head. "I understand you want to look your best at work. I can go by your place for a few minutes while you change."

After they all got in his truck, Joe drove to the hospital and parked at the entrance. His mother got out, then paused at the car's doorway. "By the way, Joe, when I took your father to the doctor last week, he confirmed your dad has Alzheimer's." She turned and walked back into the hospital.

Joe sighed. "At least she believes it now. That's a relief. Maybe she'll agree to getting some help for him at home. I'll take you to your apartment." A few minutes later, he waited in her living room while she changed.

****

Kayla was glad to be back home. Feeling grimy after their ordeal, she stripped and took a quick hot shower, then changed into a suit and blouse.

Later, after he parked in front of Brown and Leggitt, he took hold of her hand. "You look crisp and professional now, but I prefer the undressed you I saw last night." He grinned.

Kayla smiled. "Maybe you'll see me like that some evening soon."

"I'm looking forward to it, but I need to get back to the hospital." He squeezed her hand, touched his mouth with two fingers, and patted her lips. "I'll call you tonight."

Treasuring his adoring look, she walked into her office reception area. Richard Black and Thad Thayer rose to greet her.

"These men are waiting to see you," said the receptionist.

"Hello. I'm glad to see you are not shouting at each other. Thad, I don't believe we had an appointment. May I help you with something?"

Richard spoke up. "I saw you and my attorney talking to each other after the trial. Obviously, you and he are friends—" He shot her a look. "—and perhaps more than that."

"Gentlemen, stop right there. Let's talk privately in my office."

Once in her office, Thad said, "We want you to talk to Morales about that park extension bill. We'd like you to call or text him and urge him to vote against it."

"That's right," Richard said. "It will cost the taxpayers more money. Neither of us want it passed."

"Why should I? That's not what you hired me for." She shook her head. "I won't do that."

"Why not?" Thad asked. "It won't hurt to ask."

Kayla held up a finger. "First, I'm not a lobbyist.

Second, Joe Morales does not represent my district. Third, it's not my business to tell him how to vote. If that's the only reason you are here, I think you should leave. And by the way, Joe Morales is a colleague and a friend. Of course we talk. Now, you can go, both of you."

"Damn it," Richard said. "You and your crazy ideas. I told you she wouldn't help us."

"Well, it was worth a try," Thad put a hand on Richard's shoulder. "Come on, she's not going to help us."

Richard still looked sullen. "I don't know why she can't just call Morales and ask how he's going to vote."

"You're too late," Kayla snapped. "The vote was scheduled for this afternoon. It may have already passed or failed. You'll have to watch the news or read tomorrow's paper."

Richard stared at her, then faced Thad. "Is your attorney always this testy? I'm not sure I'd like that."

"Hey, she did a great job getting you to pay for my damages. Don't criticize her, cousin."

"You two are cousins?" Kayla asked.

Richard nodded. "You beat my attorney in court, but I shouldn't have to pay for a force of nature. Now I have to cough up a bunch of dough to pay for fixing that sinkhole."

Thad spoke up. "I need my half million dollars from the settlement of my case. When will I get it?"

"You'll get a check for that minus forty percent for attorney's fees," Kayla said.

Thad gasped. "That's highway robbery. I don't remember agreeing to pay you forty percent."

"You didn't have a strong case. That's why I took it on a contingency basis. You'd pay me nothing if we lost, or thirty percent if we won. However, you agreed to pay forty percent if the case had to go to court. That involves much more work and expense."

Thad shook his head. "I don't remember agreeing to that."

Kayla pulled a folder from her desk. "Here's the contract with your signature on it, plain as day."

He studied it. "Crap. I didn't pay attention to all that fine print. That will cover the cost of repair, but I'd hoped to get more for my pain and suffering like you said in court."

"I'm sorry you feel that way, but what you receive will more than cover your repairs."

Thad frowned. "I'll never hire you as my lawyer again. What's more, I'll bad-mouth you to anyone who listens."

Richard Black scowled. "I can't build any more houses until I sell all the ones I built. And it's all your fault, Ms. Walker, because you beat me in court."

She opened the door and stepped into the hallway, hoping they'd follow. "Thad, your check should be ready in a few days. Now I think you both should leave."

As they walked into the hallway, Kayla took a deep breath. Should she confront them about the kidnapping? Would that make things worse? Her heart beat faster, and she had to concentrate to breathe normally.

Laura, her attorney friend who worked in the office next to hers, came to her door. Good, she had a witness in case these men tried anything.

"By the way," she said, taking care to speak calmly, but then she paused. It might have been that guy, Carter, who ran against Joe, who arranged the kidnapping. Better not to confront these two. "Have a nice day."

"Come on, let's go," Richard said. He and Thad walked down the hall.

Thad paused and turned to face her. "Remember attorney–client privilege. If you breathe a word about what I told you about my plans, I'll not only sue you, but also make you wish you'd never met me." He turned and strode down the hall to the reception area.

Richard called after Thad. "What will you do if she talks?"

Thad beckoned Richard to come close and spoke in a low voice.

Kayla strained to hear but couldn't make out what he said. She'd wanted to get justice for him, but obviously he'd planned to harvest and sell marijuana on a large scale.

She stepped back into her office and called Joe. "How is your dad now?"

"They said he had a mild heart attack, but he's holding his own and not likely to die now."

"I hope he'll be okay soon."

"Thanks."

"Did you find out how the vote went?"

"Not yet. I'll call you back."

After he disconnected, she got busy with some work on her desk. Finally, he called. "The vote has been postponed until Monday. If my father is well enough that I feel I can leave him, I'll rent a car and drive down Monday morning. I don't want to leave town any sooner than I have to while my father's in the hospital. Would you like to take a day off and come with me? You can watch the legislature in action. Afterward we can go out to dinner and maybe take in a movie."

"That sounds great. I need to get my car and bring it

back to Dallas."

"Can we leave at five thirty?"

"Five thirty a.m.?"

"It will take us most of four hours to get there and park."

"You took me to dinner at Outback. How about having dinner at my place tonight?"

"That sounds good, but don't go to any trouble. I can't stay long because I'll need to go back to the hospital."

Kayla disconnected. At least she wouldn't have to wonder if Joe wanted to spend the night with her. As much as she wanted to share that with him, she'd feel better about being with him after the last case they had together was settled.

Now, what on earth could she fix for dinner? She wanted to fix something special. She wasn't a fantastic cook, but she could do spaghetti and a salad.

After leaving the office, she picked up a bottle of wine, salad fixings, and a can of crescent rolls.

At her place, she changed into a rust-colored dress she knew looked good on her, then set the table and put water to boiling. She mixed a salad and put it into bowls, then put rolls in the oven. She got out a big onion. As she chopped it, she brushed tears from her eyes, hoping that her eyes were not red. As soon as the ground beef started turning brown, she added the onions, minced some garlic, and threw that in also. A few minutes later, while inhaling the aroma, she added tomato sauce to the meat and dropped the spaghetti noodles into the boiling water.

The doorbell sounded, so she turned down the heat and went to the door with a spring in her step.

Joe was there, dressed in a navy blazer, a blue sports

shirt, navy pants, and a big smile. "You look marvelous."

That made her smile.

His eyes twinkling, he held out his arms and pulled her close for a kiss. His lips welcomed her and set her heart beating faster. She couldn't help but respond. He placed kisses on her forehead and her cheek.

Moving a few inches back, she smiled. "Come on in. I'm cooking spaghetti. I'd better check on it." She rushed into the kitchen and peered into the spaghetti pot. "Thank goodness, the noodles were still simmering." She turned down the heat.

He stood beside her. "That's good. How's your arm?"

"It's getting better and doesn't hurt as much. If you'll pour the wine, I'll bring the plates in." She took out the rolls, put them in a basket, and set it on the table. She dished up the spaghetti and meat sauce, then carried the plates to the table, the aroma of beef and tomato sauce wafting in the air. After they sat, she offered a brief blessing and passed the roll basket.

Joe bit into a roll, chewed it, and ate a forkful of spaghetti. All the while he ate, he kept looking at her and smiling. He had introduced her to his parents as his girlfriend. Hopefully, he cared about her as much as she did for him.

He touched her left arm, warming it. "This is delicious. You're a good cook."

She smiled. "Thank you." It was nice to get a compliment, even on a thrown-together meal.

"And not only that, you're a good person. I admire the way you fight for your clients. You care about the environment—enough to take part in a march. However, I bet you didn't expect that to result in so much pain."

She shook her head. "No, I didn't, but I'd do it again. People need to consider how our actions affect our planet. I read in the National Geographic how global warming is affecting the Arctic with the permafrost melting and making the ground collapse. Animals have a hard time finding food, but beavers have moved in and are damming up the rivers."

"Wow. I guess even a few degrees rise in temperature makes a big difference."

After they finished eating, Joe said, "Let me help you with the dishes." He carried plates to the kitchen and dried the pots and pans after she washed them. As she scrubbed at the frying pan, he grasped her shoulders and kissed the back of her neck, sending heat to her heart.

She let go of the frying pan and turned to kiss him.

His mouth was warm and welcoming. He pulled her closer against his firm chest and hugged her. Then, his hands caressed her breasts, sending tingles that radiated to her core.

He looked her in the eyes. "I wish I could stay longer. I'd like to kiss you all over."

Just thinking about it thrilled her. She met his gaze. Was he interested in being with her for more than a few nights?

He glanced at his watch. "I'd better get back to the hospital. I can't really tell if my dad's getting better. I need to try to talk to his doctor at evening rounds."

"I'm sorry. That must cause you a lot of worry."

He nodded and headed for the door. "I'll call you tomorrow."

She followed. He stopped at the door, took her in his arms, and hugged her. His kiss was warm and sexy. His tongue roved her mouth, and then he backed away a couple of inches and smiled. "Pleasant dreams." He opened the door and walked out, leaving the air cooler with his absence.

She shut the door and put on the latch. The next time he was here at night, she'd offer to share her bed. Even if they didn't last as a couple, she wanted to lie in his arms and enjoy him. That decided, she finished scrubbing the frying pan and set it in the dish drainer. She couldn't wait until Monday morning when they'd drive to Austin together. Luckily, she had no court dates.

Saturday, she picked up a new phone and was able to have Beth reschedule her Monday appointments. Drat, now she'd have to enter her contact numbers all over again.

Joe called from the hospital. "Dad's holding his own. They put in a stent to improve his circulation. When he came to, he was able to talk to me, and he even made sense."

"That's good. Maybe the Alzheimer's isn't as bad as you thought."

"I can only hope it progresses slowly."

Sunday, Joe called again. "I can't talk long. I'm trying to catch up at my office before going back to the hospital. I think they'll let Dad go home tomorrow."

"I bet you're relieved."

"Well, he's not out of the woods yet. I'm hiring someone to care for him and be sure he doesn't try to leave the house."

"What did your mother say to that?"

"She said it wasn't necessary, but she seemed relieved when I insisted. Are you still game to go with me on Monday?"

"Yes, but I'm not looking forward to getting up so

early. See you then."

She set her alarm and went to bed early. It would be good to see Joe again and get her car back from Austin.

Monday morning, after yawning and dozing on the long ride, Kayla finally climbed out of Joe's truck and picked up her car. She followed Joe downtown and parked her car near his. She walked with him toward the state capitol.

As they walked, she asked, "Did you know Richard Black and Thad Thayer are cousins?"

"No."

"They both want that park extension bill defeated. Thad fired me as his attorney because I wouldn't try to persuade you to vote against the park extension bill. He said if I broke attorney–client privilege and told anyone that, he'd sue me."

"Hey, I won't tell anyone about Thad wanting to grow weed, so don't worry about it."

"I didn't really think you would. The cousins seemed pretty adamant about not wanting that bill to pass. I suspect they hired Phil and Bill to abduct us. After I watch the legislative session, I need to report my suspicions to the Austin police. Do you think they might have put pressure on any other legislators to vote against it?"

"My friend who's afraid of blackmail is the only one I know. Richard talks a big game but doesn't always carry through, and like his cousin, he fired his attorney also."

"That's a bummer." After they walked into the pink granite capitol building, she stood in line to go through a metal detector, but Joe pulled out his handgun license and walked up to a state trooper, who inspected the

Searching for Justice

license and let him pass.

After she passed through, she asked Joe, "Can anyone with a handgun license enter the capitol building that way?"

Joe nodded. "I know some lobbyists with licenses who go through that way because it's faster. Some don't even carry their guns with them. They just want a shorter line."

She was directed to go upstairs to the gallery, and Joe went into the room for the House of Representatives. After reaching the gallery, Kayla sat in the front where she could see well.

Joe walked in and took his seat in one of the brown leather chairs in front of a wooden desk. Two large brass chandeliers hung from the ceiling with light bulbs forming a star. The bulbs in each point of the star were arranged to form letters that spelled "Texas."

As Speaker of the Texas House, her father sat at a desk at the head of the chamber. After calling the session to order, he recognized a member to speak. The representative approached the lectern in the middle of the center aisle and stated why the members should vote against the park extension bill. Some members clapped when he finished. After receiving permission, another representative walked up to the lectern and started speaking in favor of the bill.

"Stop, you can't go in there," shouted a man down below. Kayla leaned over the railing to see better.

Two men marched partway down the aisle. One shouted, "Don't pass that park bill."

Oh, my gosh. I know that voice. Why was Cash doing this?

The other man, wearing an ill-fitting blue jacket and

torn jeans, shouted, "Don't waste our money."

Kayla's father stood and pounded his gavel. "You men are out of order. Turn around immediately and leave, or the sergeant at arms will escort you out."

"We have a right to be here and speak. We don't need a bigger park," Cash said.

The speaker motioned to a man seated in the last row, who stood.

Kayla watched. Would they go peaceably?

She waited. Looked at her watch. The second hand crept around the numbers.

The man who stood, probably the sergeant at arms, walked toward them. "Please leave right now."

They argued with the sergeant.

Joe raised his hand, and the speaker nodded permission to speak. Joe strode to the lectern in the middle of the aisle.

Cash shoved the sergeant aside. Walked down the aisle and pulled out a pistol.

Chapter Thirteen

Cash pointed his gun at Joe. Kayla gasped. Her heart beat like a metronome on speed. "Joe, look out!" she shouted. She dropped to the gallery floor and pulled out her phone, fumbling to call 911. Hoped someone else had done it sooner.

From between the slats of the railing, she saw Joe pull his gun from his holster and aim it at the attackers. Kayla held her breath.

Legislators ducked down below their oak desks.

Her heart pounded. Would her father be next? Thankfully, he slid lower in his chair. A hard lump grew in her throat. How long before police came?

She held her phone to her ear. Heard it ring. She gripped the railing. Glanced at Joe. He scowled at Cash, still standing there, pointing his gun. Would someone shoot? Her pulse raced.

Cash pulled the trigger. A shot rang out. The noise echoed off the walls.

Joe's arm jerked back. "Damn," Joe yelled and returned fire.

Kayla held her breath. Cash shrieked, grabbed his side, and collapsed. The other man aimed at Joe but didn't shoot.

A representative on the right shot at the jeans-clad attacker. The representative missed, but the attacker shot him. The representative collapsed, falling over his chair.

By the time the 911 responder answered, Kayla let out the breath she'd been holding. She strained to hear.

"What is your situation?"

"People are shooting. At the capitol. In the Texas House."

"I will dispatch officers. Does anyone need medical help?"

"Legislators have been shot. Send paramedics."

"Stay out of the line of fire, but please stay connected."

Kayla shoved her phone in her pocket and peered through the railing. Those men below were not interested in her, but her stomach churned. Representatives scooted down in their seats, but all eyes faced the aisle. How many people would be shot before police came? Would anyone die?

Down below, Joe stood with his gun pointed at the attacker still standing.

Lying in the aisle, Cash grabbed his left side. "Damn you dirty politician."

Thank goodness, he was immobilized now.

Or was he? Cash lugged his gun up with his right hand but seemed to have difficulty aiming it. Oh, yes. He was left-handed.

Would either man shoot Joe again? Or hit anyone else? Kayla's hand went to her chest. She didn't want Joe to die. She hadn't realized how much she cared until now. She loved him, loved him with all her heart. With him gone, she'd have a hole inside.

She wished she had a gun. She felt helpless.

A representative on the left side of the aisle stood. He pointed a gun at the men in the aisle. "Texans don't take kindly to interfering with legislators. Put down your guns, or we'll take justice into our own hands."

Two male representatives on the right side stood and pointed guns, too. "Shoot again," one said, "and we'll blow your brains out."

A female representative pulled the fallen representative upright in his chair. She pressed a handkerchief to his wound. Kayla hoped he wasn't badly injured.

"Put down those guns," shouted a police officer she could just barely see below the gallery.

Two male officers with guns pointed walked toward Cash and his accomplice. "Put your weapons down."

Slowly, the attackers laid their guns on the floor. The legislators with guns tucked them into holsters but remained standing.

"You're under arrest. Put your hands behind you," one officer ordered.

Cash Carter clutched his side. "I've been shot. You've got to take me to the hospital."

The other officer kicked the weapons aside. "After you answer a few questions, we'll take you to the hospital for first aid."

Slowly, both attackers complied, and the officers cuffed them. The police walked the two men out of the room, reading them their rights.

Kayla sat down, her pulse still racing.

Two paramedics rushed down the aisle and tended to the wounded statesman. They placed him onto a gurney.

"Get well soon, Tom," her father said.

Others spoke encouragingly, then clapped as the paramedics wheeled him down the aisle.

Her father stood and pounded a gavel. "In view of

what's happened, I am suspending this session. We will resume where we left off at ten o'clock tomorrow."

Kayla rushed down to the ground level to wait for Joe. Off to one side, police were talking with the handcuffed attackers. After most of the representatives walked out, Joe and her father stepped out together. She hugged her dad. "I'm so glad you're okay. I was afraid one of those men might kill you."

Joe faced her. "Did you worry about me? Don't I get a hug?"

"Of course. Thank you, Joe." She hugged him, then whispered, "I couldn't bear it if you were hurt badly."

Joe shook his head. "It hurts a bit, but it's only a flesh wound. I'm sure washing and bandaging it will be enough."

Her father put a hand on Joe's shoulder. "Well, honey, thanks to him and the police, I'm okay. Joe, you were brave to react so quickly."

"I couldn't let them shoot anyone else," Joe said. "I guess you don't know how fast you can act when trouble hits. I'm surprised more representatives didn't pull out their guns."

"You may have saved several lives," Kayla said. "I hope the wounded representative isn't too badly injured." Kayla touched his arm. "Were you scared?"

He patted his semi-automatic pistol. "Didn't have time to be scared. I was concentrating on hitting that bastard. I bet he's going to prison for a long time. That's the last time he throws a brick at my window."

Another paramedic walked in, scanning the room. "You've been shot," Kayla said. "Are you sure you don't need to go to the hospital?"

"Well, maybe. I need to get my wound cleaned up

and bandaged, but I don't want to go to the hospital."

The paramedic stepped closer and set a bag down. "I can take care of that."

And he did as the remaining police officer, a lean, lanky guy, questioned her father and a few other representatives. The officer took copious notes and bagged Joe's weapon for evidence. "If I need any more information, I'll call you. You may leave now, and I don't expect there will be any charges."

As the paramedic finished wrapping a bandage around his arm, Joe grinned at the officer. "That's good to hear. You need to lock these men up. Not only have they shot people in the Texas House, but I'm sure they hired those two men, Phil and Bill, who kidnapped me and Kayla and left us in a cabin near Gunter. We already reported that to the police here, so you can check with them."

Joe walked away from the officers and their captives and joined Kayla and her father. "Now let's all go for a drink. I know the best place."

Her father shook his head. "It's been an exhausting day. I think I'll go back to my apartment and order takeout. You two enjoy yourselves. Joe, I'll see you tomorrow at the capitol. Good night."

"See you later, Dad," Kayla said.

The restaurant Joe took her to had pink flowering vines hanging down over white-painted brick. The blue sign above had the name Ah Sing Den in Chinese letters as well as English.

"They named Ah Sing Den after a famous London opium den frequented by Charles Dickens and Arthur Conan Doyle," Joe said. "I think people like it so much for the romantic history."

A waiter showed them to a small, round table set among curved velvet banquettes and low-slung purple chairs.

"I can see why," Kayla said, sinking into the wicker-style chair Joe held out for her.

A blue peacock statue peeked from nearby philodendrons.

"You've got to try one of their exotic drinks," Joe said.

She studied the menu. "Frozen vacation in a glass with vodka, coconut, pineapple, and orange sounds good. I'll try the Climate Change."

Joe ordered the exotic cocktail she'd chosen and a beer for himself.

After a server brought the drinks, he asked, "Would you like something to eat? We have chicken and shrimp dumplings."

"I want to try those shrimp dumplings," Kayla said.

They placed their orders, chicken and pork dumplings for him and shrimp dumplings for her. While they waited, he asked, "So, other than the case we have in common, how are things going at work?"

"The head partner is always after me to rack up more billable hours. I don't get the bigger cases, but having to share a paralegal with another attorney keeps me busy with the small cases. But I don't want to bore you with mundane talk about work."

Joe leaned closer. "I can understand your frustration. If you want to vent, I can listen."

Wow, a guy who will listen instead of trying to fix my problems. Who'd have thought he'd do that? "I'd like a smaller firm where there isn't so much pressure. Talk about pressure, you got it in spades today at the capitol.

I'm so glad you didn't get badly hurt. That was scary for a while."

"Well, at least no one got seriously injured, and they arrested the shooters. I didn't think Carter would stoop to that, but I hope they catch Phil and Bill and give Carter the maximum sentence."

Joe sat beside her and held her hand until their food arrived. The dumplings were different and tasty, but Joe whispered to her while they were eating. "This isn't quite as good as your spaghetti. I could eat at your place any night."

She smiled. "Thanks."

It was six o'clock when they finished. Joe paid the bill, led her out to his car, and opened the door.

After he got behind the wheel, he turned to her. "Wouldn't you rather spend the night at the apartment I've rented here while the legislature is in session? It will be an awfully long drive back to Dallas in the dark. Besides, I'd love to snuggle up beside you in bed tonight."

She'd wanted to sleep with him, and here was her chance, but she needed to be at work tomorrow. She laid her hand on his. "I'd love to, but I have to get back. I have a court hearing in the afternoon. Even though I have everything ready, I want to take time to review it in the morning."

Joe sighed. "Okay. We can spend the night together some other time, but I'll have a hard time waiting. I'll drive you to your car."

Once there, he kissed her long and hard. During her three hours on the road, Kayla kept replaying the events at the capitol over and over—the look on Joe's face— was he thinking he was facing his last moment on earth?

She'd almost had a heart attack waiting to see if someone got killed. After trudging to her apartment door with barely enough energy to get undressed, she fell into bed and slept.

All the next day, Joe didn't call. Perhaps he knew she was busy and held off. By Wednesday, he still hadn't called. She thought he'd at least let her know how the vote went. Maybe he was just interested in sex, but not a more lasting relationship. If so, it was better she hadn't slept with him again, but it would have been wonderful. Should she call or text him?

No. She'd wait. She might be reading something into the situation. Maybe he was extra busy at work, or his father might be worse.

****

Joe gathered up his notes. He was glad the park extension bill had passed. He was thrilled that David Walker appointed him head of the committee to make up regulations concerning the expanded park. All day yesterday and this morning, the legislature had argued about other bills. Now he'd spent all this afternoon getting the members of both parties to agree on them.

He was glad to have a breather, so he could call Kayla. She must think he'd forgotten about her. Sure was hard to keep up a relationship with him being in Austin so much. He hoped, with her father in the legislature, she wasn't surprised that Joe had to be away a lot.

She answered his call on the first ring. "Hi, haven't heard from you in a while."

"It's good to hear your voice. I'm sorry I haven't called, but I've been really busy. Until your dad appointed me in charge of the park extension, I never realized how much work a committee chairman does, and I've been busy dealing with my father."

"I see. Is he doing okay now?"

"Yes. He's home and seems to be recovering. I got Mom to agree to have help. I was also busy arranging the home healthcare. Nurse Powell will take care of Dad and make sure he doesn't leave the house."

"I'm glad you've got that set up. Bet that takes a load off your mind. When will you be back in Dallas?"

"Not until Thursday evening. I'll call you when I arrive. I can't wait to see you again." As soon as he said it, he realized how true it was. She was special. He missed being with her, missed seeing her smiling face and talking to her.

"I've missed you, too."

"If we can have the Witherspoons sign the divorce decree Friday, I'd like to take you out to celebrate that evening. Now that it's almost finalized, we don't have to worry about being seen together."

Kayla laughed. "It's bad when someone else's divorce comes between us. Why don't you see if you can talk your client into being reasonable about paying for four years of college for his wife so she can be self-supporting?"

"I'll see what I can do. Talk to you later."

Joe couldn't wait to touch her and caress her lovely body all over, something he could see himself doing for months and maybe years. What would it be like to have her share all of his life?

****

All day Friday, Kayla hurried through her work. She couldn't stop thinking about Joe coming to see her tonight.

This afternoon, she and Joe were meeting with the

Witherspoons in the conference room in his office to discuss the final divorce decree.

She checked her personal e-mail on her phone and opened a notice regarding the last job opening she'd applied for. "We regret to inform you the position you were interested in has been filled." Kayla grimaced. A wave of disappointment washed over her. Then she straightened her shoulders. She wouldn't let that ruin her day. *Somewhere, somehow, there was a better place for her.* Pasting a smile on her face, she said goodbye to Beth and left for the meeting.

Seated in the Larson and Morales conference room with Rose, she assembled her notes and the copy of the divorce decree Beth had prepared according to Rose Witherspoon's wishes. Hopefully, Larry Witherspoon would agree.

Joe and Mr. Witherspoon walked in. Joe wore a gray pinstripe suit and lavender tie. She loved seeing a sharply dressed man. His smile welcomed her, but he was all business as he set out his copy of a decree and showed his client to a seat. "I have discussed the terms with my client, and I hope we can come to an agreement." He passed a copy to Kayla.

Kayla handed Larry and Joe her copy of the decree. For a moment, all was quiet except for the squawk of crows outside. Then Mr. Witherspoon slapped his hand on the table. "I'm not agreeing to pay for four years of college. I agreed to pay for three years."

Kayla studied Joe's copy of the divorce decree. Joe must have kept his promise and talked to Larry about it, because the decree said three years instead of two, but she was going to fight for more.

Frowning, Larry continued. "Rose can get a nursing

degree in three years. She doesn't need to get a full four-year degree to support herself."

Kayla concentrated on keeping her tone even. "Even with you paying child support, don't you want Rose to be eligible for better-paying positions which she'd get with more education? That way, Sally will be well supported, and there will be enough money for Rose to save for your daughter's college in the future."

"Oh," Mr. Witherspoon said. "I hadn't thought that far ahead. I suppose Sally will want to go to college."

Kayla leaned forward. "Then, for Sally's sake, will you agree to pay for four years of college for Rose and half of Sally's college if she goes?"

Still frowning, he nodded.

"I'll agree to that," Rose said.

Joe wrote on Kayla's copy and headed for the door. "I'll have Anne type this up."

Rose sat beaming beside Kayla. She focused on her husband. "Thank you, Larry. I really appreciate this. Now Sally will be well provided for."

A few minutes later, Joe returned with two copies of a document and gave them to Larry and Rose, who held it so Kayla could read it.

Joe handed Mr. Witherspoon a pen. "If this meets with Rose's and your approval, will you sign it now?" He glanced at Kayla and Rose.

Kayla carefully scrutinized the decree and glanced at Rose, who nodded. "This will be fine."

After they both signed, Joe said, "I'll arrange the final hearing and notify you and Mrs. Witherspoon."

Kayla drew a sigh of relief. At least this matter was concluded well. After saying goodbye to Rose, she walked to her car. Before getting in, she raised her fist and grinned. *I did it. I got what I wanted for my client despite the husband's opposition.* This case certainly ended on a high note.

Kayla refrained from checking her e-mail again for news on her job quest, but she'd keep looking. Surely, someone would be interested in having her work for them. She looked forward to Joe taking her out tonight.

Later, while she shed her suit and was getting ready to go out with Joe, she thought about him. He was smart, caring, thoughtful, and he "got" her. He was everything she'd want in a man.

She really cared for him, and he'd done his best to get his client to agree to the more equitable settlement for his wife and daughter. She hoped Joe's father's dementia wasn't getting any worse.

Kayla had bought a new dress, gold with embossed golden heart shapes circling the neckline. It clung to her curves. She hoped he liked it. Dabbing perfume over her neck, she inhaled the gardenia smell.

Since their clients' case was resolved, neither of them had to hold off. Would Joe want to spend the night? She was more than ready to be close with him again. Just the thought of it set her heart beating faster.

When the doorbell rang, she hurried to let him in. Still wearing his sharp gray suit that emphasized his large chest and broad shoulders, he took one look and said, "Wow." He hugged and kissed her. "You smell great. I'm taking you to Outback for a big steak or whatever you want. I can't wait to walk in with you by my side."

She smiled. "Thank you, kind sir," she said with a slight bow. "I'll get my jacket."

As he helped her into her jacket, he kissed her neck.

She tilted her head toward him, savoring the feel of his lips on her skin. He squeezed her shoulders, making her feel like falling into his arms right now.

"Let's go, gorgeous."

At the restaurant, he held her hand while the aroma of steaks cooking wafted by. After they ordered, a server brought salads.

"So, how was the rest of your day?" Joe asked.

"Fine, except I got another 'sorry, the position's filled' letter."

He placed his hand over hers. "That's too bad. I can't imagine a law firm not wanting someone as well prepared for arguing in court as you are. We'll have to order dessert to sweeten up your day." His phone dinged, announcing a text message. "Would you excuse me for a moment? I have to make a call." He left the table and walked outside.

Hungry, she ate most of the brown loaf the server had brought. What was taking him so long?

Joe returned just as their steaks arrived. "Guess you sometimes have to take care of business after hours. I needed to confer with Matt about something."

Glad they got along well enough to talk about business even after hours, she sliced off a bite of steak and enjoyed its juicy flavor.

For dessert, they shared Chocolate Thunder from Down Under, a pecan brownie topped with vanilla ice cream and warm chocolate sauce. While drinking coffee, Joe said, "I have two propositions for you."

"Go on. I'm intrigued."

"And I can't wait to tell you." He stood and waved to someone.

A minute later, Matt Larson stood beside their table.

"Hello, Kayla." He pulled out a chair and sat. "I know this is a celebratory dinner, so I won't take much of your time. Joe and I believe we could use another attorney. After the workout you put Joe through with those two cases, we feel a lawyer who is strong in court would be an asset. Would you like to work with us? As a partner, of course. We can talk about the financials involved later."

Kayla's mouth dropped open, but she quickly shut it. This was the answer to her dreams, a small firm with people she enjoyed working with. Her pulse racing, she took a deep breath and smiled. "I'd love to."

Matt shook her hand. "I can't wait until you give notice and come join us. With your reputation after winning the sinkhole case, we should get a lot more business. Let us know when you can move in."

"I will. And thanks, Matt." She turned to Joe. "And thank you, too."

"Hear, hear. This calls for a drink." Joe ordered three glasses of champagne, which the waiter brought.

Lifting his glass, he clinked it against Matt's and Kayla's. "Here's to Larson, Morales, and Walker. May they win all their cases."

"Or at least ninety percent of them," Matt said. "Let's be realistic."

"Well," Kayla said, "our aim is to win all of them, but I can accept ninety percent."

Matt finished his wine and rose. "I'll leave you two to finish your coffee. See you Monday, Joe. And Kayla, I'm looking forward to your moving in as soon as possible."

"I second that," Joe said.

As he walked away, Kayla took another deep breath.

"This is wonderful. I can hardly believe it."

Joe nodded. "Matt is a tough taskmaster, but I've seen you in action. I know you'll fit right in."

They drank the rest of their wine. Joe gave the server his credit card and directed him to add a generous tip. After signing the slip, Joe led Kayla out to his car. "That steak was good, but I ate so much, I could use a short stroll in the park to let it settle."

"I'd love a stroll. Let's go." Kayla gathered her purse and wrap.

He drove to Josey Lane, then pulled into Mallon Park. He stopped the car and opened the door for Kayla.

Taking her hand, he strolled with her across a bridge over a creek, then walked back with her to a set of swings with long wooden slats. "Want me to push you?"

Kayla shook her head. "I just want to sit here and enjoy the view." She pushed off with her foot so the swing moved a little, then sat still. "I'm enjoying the breeze."

"And I enjoy just being with you."

"Joe, you mentioned you have two propositions. What's the second one?"

"I'm glad you remembered." He walked around in front of her and got down on one knee. Holding a small gray box in one hand, he held out his other hand to her. "Kayla, we've been through so much together—me pulling you out of the sinkhole, a kidnapping, a tornado, and the shooting at the capitol—enough that I know I love you and want you to be my lifetime partner and my wife."

Kayla smiled. What could she say but yes? "Yes, I'd love that, and I love you, too."

With a big grin on his face, Joe jumped up and

pulled her from the swing. He hugged and kissed her.

The kiss was long and heavenly. She put her arms around his neck and kissed him again. "Are you going to show me the ring?"

Joe laughed. "I almost forgot about that. Hearing you say yes made me so happy it slipped my mind, but thank goodness, I didn't drop the box." He backed off enough to open the box so she could see a circle of glittering sparkle, topped by a large gleaming diamond. He slipped it on her finger, and it fit perfectly.

"I'll wear it with pride and cherish it because you gave it to me."

He put his arm around her. "Let me take you home now. I'd better spend the night so no burglars will disturb you."

She looked him in the eyes. "And might you have another reason for that?"

He nodded. "I want to make love to my future wife, the most wonderful woman in the world." He took her in his arms.

Kayla smiled. Her dream of a partner in law and life was coming true. What more could she ask for, except perhaps sunshine on her wedding day?

Dear Reader,

If you enjoyed Searching for Justice, I'd love for you to write a review and post it on Amazon.

Check my website, Carolynrae.com and Facebook Page, Carolyn Rae Author for news of new books, excerpts, and to sign up for my newsletter.

A word about the author…

As a teenager, Carolyn Rae told stories to kids she babysat. On a long road trip, she entertained her younger sister with stories she made up.

Later she taught home economics and family living in Michigan, Illinois, and Texas, where she earned a master's degree and also taught English. In Illinois, she worked as a researcher for a mincemeat company and met her neighbors by bringing samples of mincemeat pies. She was a teacher and supervisor of ironwork, painting, and carpentry residents at the Fort Worth Federal Correctional Institution in Texas. While there, she also wrote and directed videos on nutrition and fair fighting for married couples

Carolyn Rae wrote the text and many recipes for There IS Life After Lettuce (Eakin Press, Fort Worth), a cookbook for heart patients and diabetics. Her profile and travel articles have appeared in the Romance Writer's Report, Fort Worth Star Telegram, The Dallas Morning News, Positive Parenting, and AAA World, Hawaii and Alaska. She has worked as a paralegal and follows her passion, writing romantic suspense where bullets are flying, people are dying, and lovers are resisting attraction until they can escape the danger following them.

http://carolynrae.com

Thank you for purchasing
this publication of The Wild Rose Press, Inc.

For questions or more information
contact us at
info@thewildrosepress.com.

The Wild Rose Press, Inc.
www.thewildrosepress.com

www.ingramcontent.com/pod-product-compliance
Lightning Source LLC
Chambersburg PA
CBHW060053260626

47160CB00005B/1665